"What are you talking about?" I demanded. "What's wrong with Rea?"

"You *know* her?" Cass chirped. I explained that we were lab partners in Ms. Llord's class, and Munch's new friends exchanged looks. "Oh," Cass then went. "So it's not like you're friends or anything, then. That's a relief."

Vi was still staring at Rea's back in a way that made me feel really uncomfortable. "Why shouldn't I be friends with Rea?" I asked. Once more, a knowing look flashed among the three.

"She's bad news," Vi said, stretching each word as long as she could. "Really, really baaad news."

I glanced over my shoulder again at Rea, who was eating steadily, her eyes pinned on a book she'd opened beside her tray. "She's nice, and she's really smart in biology," I protested. Looking at Vi defiantly, I added, "I *like* her."

"Oh boy," Cass murmured. "*Oh* boy. Maybe we should tell her. . . ."

By Maureen Wartski
Published by Fawcett Books:

BELONGING
DARK SILENCE
THE FACE IN MY MIRROR
CANDLE IN THE WIND
WHAT ARE THEY SAYING ABOUT ME?

WHAT ARE THEY SAYING ABOUT ME?

Maureen Wartski

FAWCETT JUNIPER • NEW YORK

A Fawcett Juniper Book
Published by Ballantine Books
Copyright © 1996 by Maureen Wartski
Excerpt from *Candle in the Wind* copyright © 1995 by Maureen Wartski

http://www.randomhouse.com

Library of Congress Catalog Card Number: 96-96355

ISBN 0-449-70451-3

Manufactured in the United States of America

First Edition: September 1996

10 9 8 7 6 5 4 3 2 1

To my good friend Tina Melcher

ACKNOWLEDGMENTS

Many thanks to Officer Robert Dixon of the Millis Police Department, to Ashley Villani for her expertise on running, and to Lynn Marie and Bert Wartski for letting me use labs from their LOW COST BIOLOGY in Ms. Llord's classroom.

ONE

SOMETHING WAS WRONG.

The house all silent, hall closet standing wide-open, my grandmother's navy blue windbreaker gone from its hook—

"Mimi?" I called.

No answer, but Gorki, who was curled up on the top of the upright piano, meowed sleepily. I checked the message taker at the foot of the stairs and got Mrs. Cruss explaining why she hadn't been able to come over this afternoon.

"Mimi, this is Regina. My daughter just called. I have to go and pick up my granddaughter at day care and take her to see the pediatrician. . . ." The rest of the message was garbled because Dad had been meaning to but hadn't gotten around to changing the old tape.

Our next-door neighbor, who was supposed to come and sit with my grandmother every afternoon till I got home from school, hadn't showed. Left alone today, Mimi had taken off.

"Why *today*?" I moaned.

Today, my impossible, disgusting, freaked-out first day at South Regional High School. I'd barely managed to drag myself home and all I wanted to do was crawl into my room, pull the covers over my head, and hide. Instead of which I had to go and find my grandmother.

Maybe she was just taking a nap? With hope springing eternal (as Mimi might say), I scooted up the stairs, down the hall to the empty bedroom next to mine.

Gorki brushed past my legs to hop onto Mimi's neatly made bed covered with her blue quilt. There she sat staring wisely at my grandmother's night table with Mimi's gazillion photographs, her latest mystery novel, and the Steuben glass vase with the white rosebud in it.

"Dad is going to go ballistic," I muttered.

The last time Mimi had wandered off was two weeks ago, and my folks had almost gone crazy before they'd found her walking aimlessly down one of the side streets. Since then, they'd had Mrs. Cruss come over afternoons to stay with her, and they'd made sure she wore an identification bracelet. "My lucky-charm bracelet," Mimi had called it, the irony of it strong in her musical voice.

If I could find her and bring her back before the folks found out, life would be a lot easier. With that in mind I headed out to the backyard and got my bike out of the toolshed.

I had a pretty good idea where Mimi'd gone. Last weekend Mom had taken time from the store so we three could have lunch at the Six Corners Mall in Chisolm. A new music store, Keyboard, had just opened next to the restaurant, and Mimi had been excited by the grand piano on display.

Be there, Mimi! I pedaled double time as I looped around Mountain Road, zipped through the busy intersection where Route 27 crosses Mountain. And I hadn't been wrong. As soon as I got inside the Six Corners Mall, I heard the soaring strains of *Rhapsody in Blue*.

2

A group of shoppers had gathered around the music store. As I made for the entrance I bumped a plump woman in pink slacks and a polyester top. She gave me a dirty look as I slid past her and then ducked around an old guy who was keeping time with both hands.

"She's good," he was saying to the person next to him. "Do you think she works for the store?"

Mimi was leaning into the music. Her eyes were closed, her gray head tipped back, and long-fingered hands danced confidently over the keys. My heart swelled with exasperation and pride as I watched Margaret S. Castleway making old Gershwin sing.

A small, pink, nervous-looking man was hovering close to the piano. He had "store manager" written all over his face, so I walked over to him. "Hi," I said. "I'm Meg Fairling. That's my grandmother playing the piano."

Relief brightened his eyes. "Aha," he went. "She just, you know, walks in, sits down, and begins to play." He added, "She's, ah, very good."

"Mimi used to be a music teacher," I told him. "She's played with the Blakewood Civic Symphony and the Moorlake Community Orchestra. She, uh, sometimes sees a piano she likes and sits down to try it out."

I figured that sounded pretty reasonable, but the store manager only said, "You certainly got here fast. I only phoned the number on her bracelet five minutes ago and Wellford's quite a hike."

He'd already called my folks at the store. My heart sank, but then I thought that if I could get Mimi out of Keyboard before they arrived, it mightn't be so bad. I walked over to my grandmother and put a hand on her shoulder. "Hey there," I told her. "It's time to go home."

3

She didn't hear me. Lines of concentration creased her forehead, her eyes were closed, and she swayed with the only thing real to her—the music. "Mimi," I said louder, "Mom and Dad are coming to get you. We need to go meet them."

"Coming to hear me play? How nice," my grandmother murmured. She still didn't open her eyes. "But the concert may be over by then. When will they be here, Meg?"

"We have to go, Mimi." I gave her shoulder a little shake. "Don't give me a rough time today, okay? It's been pure hell."

"The road to hell is paved with good intentions." My grandmother shook back feathery gray wisps of hair and added pensively, "I'm sure they *meant* to be here on time."

I noted that Mimi's audience was eagerly listening in on our conversation and that the store manager was beginning to chew his lip and tap his foot. Having some weird lady glued to his piano could prove bad for business no matter how well she played.

"Mimi," I cajoled, "listen to me, okay? If Dad and Mom find you here, it's not going to be a good scene. We have to leave now."

She opened her eyes and gave me a surprised, deep violet look. "What's the matter? You sound upset."

"I *am* upset. Mimi, we have to get out of here."

Too late. Out of the tail of my eye I saw Dad striding into the store. He looked grim.

I tugged on Mimi's arm, causing her to miss a few notes. "That," she said irritably, "was impolite. Don't you young people have any manners?"

4

Before I could answer, Dad bore down on us. "All right, Mother," he said grimly, "it's time to leave."

Dad's balding forehead was wet with perspiration, and behind his shades I knew that his eyes would be as angry as his voice. Behind him, Mom looked worried and frazzled. "There you are, Mama," she said in a too-bright voice.

Mimi folded her hands in her lap, and her violet-blue eyes now held a bewildered but stubborn expression. "I can't go yet, Nolly. I haven't finished my recital."

Ignoring her, Dad began to talk to the store manager. Mom slid a plump arm around Mimi. "Meg," she directed me, "take her other arm, and let's get her to the car."

"Do not go gentle into that good night," Mimi advised. Then she commenced to whistle Gershwin.

As we led her out the fat woman with the polyester top said loudly, "Probably Alzheimer's, poor thing. Me, I'd rather take a pill."

I glared at her, hoping Mimi hadn't heard, but she just continued to whistle.

"Mama, how could you?" My mom sighed. "You promised." Mimi whistled on. "You just can't keep *doing* this. Jerry and I had to close the store, and—Mama, do you hear me?"

She finally got through. Mimi quit her whistling and looked guilty. "Sorry," she muttered. "I'm sorry, Nolly."

By now, Dad had joined us. "What are we going to do with her?" he asked Mom over Mimi's head. "We can't keep chasing her all over the county." He yanked the car door open with such force that the hinges screeched. "Damn. *Damn* it. What happened to that Cruss woman?" I explained about the phone message, and Dad swore

5

again. "You'll have to stay at home with her today," he told Mom. "We can't risk her wandering off again."

"I'll take care of her," I said quickly.

"This is the fourth time this month, for God's sake," Dad fumed.

"Jerry, *please*."

Mimi looked apprehensively from Dad to Mom and then back again. "I did something stupid again. I'm sorry."

She sounded bewildered. Mom looked ready to cry. "It's okay, Mama," she said. "Jerry's just worried about you. Now get in the car, okay? Meg, did you bike down here? Help your grandmother in, then go get your bike."

Mimi was really quiet as I helped her in. Her usually agile, wire-slender body seemed suddenly awkward, and she kept looking at Dad apprehensively.

It was like this whenever she had her confused spells. Sometimes she blinked at people she'd known for years as if trying to remember whether she'd ever seen them before. Sometimes she would repeat one word over and over, then shake her head in despair. Or, like now, she'd sit looking so bewildered and unhappy that my stomach ached for her.

This was Margaret Singingtree Castleway, for whom I was named. At five-seven we stood nose to nose, and her genes had marked me in other ways. We had the same short torso, long legs, wide mouth, high cheek-bones, and the blue-black hair that had come down from my Navaho great-grandmother. Only our eyes were distinct from each other's, mine being gray like Dad's, hers, wild-violet blue.

Those eyes followed me as I secured my bike on the

6

bike rack in back of the car. "I did something stupid, didn't I, Meg?" she questioned.

I wanted to cry. Mimi was the smartest woman I'd ever known. She'd taught music, written an opera, read a million books. When she was my age, she'd trekked all over Europe and climbed the Matterhorn. She'd freedom-marched to Washington and played the piano for the Reverend Martin Luther King, Jr.

"No," I told her around the thick lump in my throat, "you didn't do anything stupid. You're just fine, Mimi," I added forcefully. "You really are."

But she was still worried. "It's really all right?"

"Sa' *right.*"

I held up a hand for her tentative high five. In the front seat, Dad mumbled something. "Jerry," Mom said, sharp under her breath, "we'll discuss it *later.*"

My folks didn't speak another word until we'd reached the house. Then Dad unlocked his lips to ask me if I could manage. "We closed the store at the busiest time of the day," he said stiffly. "We have to get back there *if* we want to stay in business."

I said we'd be fine and led Mimi into the house. Once there, she seemed to draw a mental breath. "I can *manage,*" she said.

Sliding her arm out of mine, she climbed the stairs to her room. I was debating whether or not I should follow her when the phone started to ring. I snatched up the receiver and my best friend, Karen, sang into the receiver, "Hey, Megs! I had to stay after and talk to one of my teachers, so I got to take the late bus home. Bum-*mer.* Did you survive our first day, or what?"

Feeling suddenly exhausted, I collapsed onto a stool by the phone. Mimi's problems had made me forget the

7

first half of my day, but now it came flooding back in all its awfulness.

"Munch," I reported, "I have Ms. Llord for biology."

"Omigod," Karen screamed. "Oh, no. I'd kill myself."

Even before we got to South Regional, that humongous high school to which the towns of Moorlake, Chisolm, and Rentown and Wellford all sent their young, there'd been rumors about Ms. Ada Llord. In Moorlake Middle School we'd heard how "Lord Doom" had terrorized generations of freshmen, learned that even the principal at South Regional, Mr. MacMasters, gave Ms. Llord plenty of room.

None of the rumors had been false. Today, on the first day of school, Ms. Llord had assigned us seats, made us sign student contracts on appropriate classroom behavior, and given us a test.

"Get out," Karen moaned. "A *test* on the first day of school?"

"She said she wanted to 'ascertain what we didn't know.' And that's not all, Munch! After the test, she assigned us two chapters to read and about fifty questions to answer, none of which I've done because Mimi got confused and—"

There was a thumping sound from upstairs. I told Karen I'd talk to her later and raced up the stairs in time to catch Gorki hightailing it out of Mimi's room. Inside the room, my grandmother stood by the bedside table, staring floorward. "The cat knocked over my photographs," she told me sadly.

She made no effort to help me when I began to gather up the photographs. Instead, she sat down on the bed and watched me. After a while she began to point to the photographs.

8

"My older brother, Tom," she told me. "That's Aunt Betty. She made the best rhubarb cobbler in the county. Did I ever tell you that she gave me the recipe? Caused a rift in the entire family. My cousin Irene Killingforth won't talk to me because Aunt Betty didn't give *her* the recipe. I really should give it to Irene one of these days."

Irene Killingforth had died ten years ago, and I'd heard the story a hundred times. I grunted noncommittally and placed another photo on the table.

"Ned," she murmured with pleasure. "My husband. Do you know him?" Insides knotting with a familiar unhappiness, I nodded. "But of course you do," she then said, surprising me with a sudden moment of clarity. "You were Papa Ned's golden girl. He called you 'Leggy Meg' because you were all legs."

"Yeah," I said enthusiastically, trying to draw her back out of the shadows. "You used to play the piano for us and we'd dance, Papa and me. Remember? You used to play Sousa and Gershwin, like you did this afternoon."

"This afternoon?" Mimi sounded bewildered.

"Yes," I said, holding her lovely amethyst eyes with mine. *Stay with me, Mimi.* "At the mall, remember? You had all the shoppers standing around listening while you played that piano at Keyboard."

Mimi shook her head, frowning. "Why would I play a piano in a mall?" she asked me. "We have a perfectly good one in the living room, and—oh, dear!"

Painfully, she bent down and picked up another photo in its frame. "Look," she said sadly.

The crack in the glass traveled diagonally across the picture of a smiling, younger Mimi. Behind that jagged fracture, the high-cheekboned photographed face smiled

9

confidently. My grandmother looked at it, her own eyes troubled.

"It's all blowing away like sand," she told me sadly. "All blowing away."

TWO

NEXT MORNING I slept through the alarm clock, Mom's waking me twice, and her final decree that if I didn't get myself out of bed, I was going to miss the bus. When I finally did open my eyes, the snooze alarm was running out of steam, and I had four minutes to make the bus.

Mr. Conyers, the girls' track coach at Moorlake Middle School, would've been proud of the speed I clocked running to the bus stop. Unfortunately, it was a total waste of time. The bus had long since come and gone, and so had my parents, who'd left for the store. I was in the back getting my bike out of the toolshed when Mimi leaned out of the back door. "Missed your bus, eh?" she called.

She sounded fine. Her blue-violet eyes—Liz Taylor eyes, my grandpa had called them—were sparkling as if she found the situation funny. She *looked* like the old Mimi.

"Yup," I said cautiously. "I'm taking my bike."

"Chisolm's quite a distance." She reached down to pick up Gorki and cuddle her. "Better get going to school or your goose is pissed."

When she said that, I felt like singing and dancing

11

because I knew she really was okay. Mimi enjoyed Regency novels, and she liked using the salty nineteenth-century sayings to get a rise out of people. But then, as I was pedaling away from the house and down woodsy Fern Way, I wondered if she'd be clear in her mind when I got back from school or as confused as she'd been yesterday.

But there was no use borrowing trouble because plenty of real grief was waiting just ahead. The south section of Chisolm, where South Regional High School had been built, *was* a hike. I'm no slouch on a bike, but by the time I arrived, first period was almost over.

I had to get a late pass from the office, where a mean-looking lunk I remembered from Ms. Llord's class was waiting to see the principal, and blew into English in the middle of a lecture about George Orwell. Then, as I was sifting through my notes, I realized I'd forgotten my biology homework at home.

I was history. I was *gone*. So scared that I felt dizzy, I tried to think of what I could do. Should I go to the nurse and say I was sick? Or maybe I could forge my folks' signature on a dismissal note. Munch'd done it before, but I never had, and—no, face it, Meg, there was only one thing *to* do.

I was frantically scribbling when the buzzer announced the end of English and left me to face biology with only half of my homework finished. Racing to Ms. Llord's classroom, I dived into my seat and began scribbling again.

Other kids came in, but I paid no attention until a cloud of heavy perfume drifted past me. I glanced up and noted that a girl was arranging her books on the desk next to mine. She was an inch or two shorter than I was, and she had on a dark skirt and a cream-colored blouse that made me feel scruffy in my torn-at-the-knees blue jeans and hastily dragged-on T-shirt. Her long black hair was pulled back in a ponytail. Purplish lipstick contrasted sharply with smooth olive skin.

She caught me looking, gave me an uncertain half smile, then looked quickly away as Ms. Llord made her entrance. "Good morning, Jed Berringer," she said to a tall blond boy who'd just walked in. "Homework?"

Her voice seemed to rise from the soles of her black, high-heeled pumps. She was really tiny, but she acted as if she were seven feet tall.

"Homework, Gus Silva?"

"Oh man, oh man," I mumbled. The dark girl slanted me a curious look. "What's the answer to question sixteen?" I hissed.

Before she could answer, Ms. Llord marched over toward us. "Homework, Meg Fairling?"

Under a short cap of salt-and-pepper hair, her pale blue eyes held mine. Ignoring my feeble explanations, she collected my unfinished homework and switched her attention to my neighbor. "Homework, Rea Alvarez?"

As Rea Alvarez handed a sheaf of papers to Lord Doom, she cut me another one of those slanting glances. "Sorry," she mouthed.

"Not your fault," I muttered. Then, as Ms. Llord went around naming other kids and demanding homework, I asked, "Does she know *everybody's* names already?"

Rea Alvarez rolled her eyes. "My married cousin Lucia had her a few years ago," she reported in a hushed voice. "Lucia said Ms. Llord never forgets *anything*."

"I'm busted," I moaned, which was when the bell went. As it clanged, the dude I'd seen earlier at the principal's office came strutting in.

"Hey," he announced, "I made it. Ta-daa!"

He made victory signs with both hands and waggled his knees as if he'd just made a touchdown. Ms. Llord looked at him as if she'd just discovered a toad in her classroom.

"Darryl Haas," she directed. "Sit down immediately or see me for detention."

You could see a struggle going on in Darryl Haas's broad face. For a second it looked as if he were going to give Ms. Llord some lip. Then he meekly shuffled to the seat at which she was pointing. He sat down, started to drop his books on the floor, caught her eye, and instead very carefully placed them on the desk.

I was awed. I'd seen guys like Darryl before, knew they lived to rank on kids weaker than themselves and to harass teachers. Nervously, I listened as Lord Doom declared that today we were going to learn to work with a lab partner.

She marched us across to the other side of the classroom, where the lab tables were set up, and announced that our activity would be related to element cycles. Say, what? "There are six elements necessary for life," she went on. "Since ninety-nine percent of life is composed of these elements, we will see how they move through the systems of all living things. Now, as to partners."

She commenced reeling off names. Jed Berringer, the blond boy I'd noticed earlier, got stuck with the element phosphorus and Darryl Haas. "Meg," Ms. Llord went on, "you'll work with Rea on the element sulfur."

14

We moved to a table placed under one of the huge potted plants that Ms. Llord had hanging all around the classroom, and Rea explained the instruction sheet. As she did so I realized what a prize I'd drawn. Rea was *good* at biology. She understood Ms. Llord's explanations about anaerobic and aerobic decomposition and her slim hands moved swiftly to diagram the cycle of sulfur as it moved through living creatures.

"Awesome," I gasped, and she smiled shyly, showing a dimple in her chin.

After biology came social studies and Mr. Jacobs, who was handsome enough to die for but cursed with a voice that reminded me of fingernails running up and down a blackboard. Only the thought of lunch kept me awake through his long, boring lecture on early America, and when I finally made it to the cafeteria, I found Rea Alvarez in front of me in the lunch line.

"What do you think the 'Tuesday Surprise' is?" I asked her.

"Monday's leftovers," she came right back, and we both laughed. She had pretty teeth, I noted, and her smile made her dark eyes sparkle. "I'm taking the cheese sandwich and the apple pie. You?"

Reluctantly skipping the pie—I needed to shed a couple of vacation pounds before facing tryouts for the South Regional cross-country team—I ordered a cheese sandwich and a salad. Then, as we carried our trays over to a table, I thanked her for showing me what to do in biology lab. "You'd be a great teacher," I said with enthusiasm.

Rea looked pleased. "I think that's what I'd like to do—teaching, I mean," she told me.

I told her that was great and that I myself was clueless

as to what I wanted to be. "Well, us kids *have* to know because my mother believes in everyone having a goal." Rea rolled her eyes. "Mama never went to college, so it's like, all you kids have to make something out of yourselves."

How many kids was that? I asked. "Three. Me, and my sisters Carmencita and Corazón. They're twins—second grade." Rea took a dainty bite of the cheese sandwich, which she held as carefully as she'd held the lab equipment. "Kids, eh? They want to be ballerinas this week. Last week they were going to be doctors."

When I was in second grade, I told Rea, I'd wanted to be a piano player like Mimi. But instead of nimble fingers, I'd ended up with itchy feet. "I'm into distance running," I told Rea. "Mimi's always telling me that I can play the piano *and* run, but I never seem to have the time."

"Is Mimi your older sister?"

"My grandmother. She's living with us," I explained, and Rea said so was hers.

There was real warmth in her voice. Encouraged, I said, "Mimi was a music teacher, you know? And she plays the piano real well. She reads tons of books and she likes to quote them, and she loves sports, too, especially football. She's been a Patriots fan for years. One time she climbed the Matterhorn."

Then I asked myself why I was babbling like a dork. Why should Rea, who I hardly knew, be interested in my grandmother? But instead of changing the subject Rea went, "Abuelita is a lot of fun, too. Once she gets into the mood, she's just like another kid, laughing and joking—"

She broke off, started to giggle. "What?" I asked.

16

"It's a switch, eh? The grandkids are bragging about the grandmothers." She touched a golden cross around her neck. "Abuelita gave me this necklace."

"Pretty," I admired.

"My grandpa gave it to her when he was courting her." Rea's eyes sparkled. "Abuelita used to be real pretty. Lively, too, until her arthritis in the hip got so bad. Now she can't walk without help." I said that was rough. "I walk with her every afternoon after school, and she tells me things about when she was a little girl in Puerto Rico."

She paused to give me a little grin. "Mainly, they're stories I've heard a hundred times, eh? But I pretend I've never heard them before 'cause it makes her feel good."

"Mimi doesn't—" but I broke off. I'd been about to say Mimi never repeated herself, that she had humor and vigor and could tell jokes in her lovely, musical voice until you rolled on the floor laughing.

But that was Mimi as she'd been a long time ago. I thought of the way she'd been yesterday and spoke quickly to keep the memory away.

"Where did you go to school before coming to South Regional?" I asked.

"Chisolm Middle School," Rea said.

As we cleaned and stacked our trays, Rea suddenly gave this little gasp.

She was staring at some point over my right shoulder. Surprised, I looked around and saw Munch sitting at a table on the far side of the room with two girls I didn't recognize. One girl had her strawberry-blond head turned away from us, but the other one was really dramatic looking. She wore a turquoise micromini and

17

chrome-yellow fishnet stockings, and her shoulder-length hair was so fair it was almost white. And she was tall. Next to her, Karen looked like a tanned, chubby little kid.

"The one with the short curly brown hair's my friend Karen Tierney, aka Munch," I told Rea. "I've known her since the first grade. C'mon—I want you to meet her."

But then I realized that I was talking to air. Rea had turned away and was making tracks out of the cafeteria away from me. Hadn't she heard me? I wondered.

I looked uncertainly at Karen, but she was busy talking to her two companions and hadn't even seen me. I hurried after Rea, found her walking rapidly up the corridor. "Hey," I said, "why did you take off like that?"

She said nothing. Looking at her curiously, I saw that her face had gone pale, that her lips were folded tight. "What's the matter?" I asked.

Rea glanced sideways at me, hesitated, then gave me a stiff-lipped little smile. "I guess my stomach didn't like my lunch. Maybe I should have had the Tuesday Surprise after all, eh?"

The cheese sandwich *had* been pretty lame. I said I'd see Rea later and trotted off to my fifth-period study. The rest of the day washed over me like a slow wave that carried me to the final bell, and I was thankfully heading for my bike when someone shrieked, "Megs!" and Karen came bouncing over to me.

"I saw you at lunch," she bubbled. "Why didn't you come over? The girls are so excellent, especially Diana Angeli. She's so cool."

"Is she the one with the white hair?" I asked.

18

"No, that's Vi. Vi Rochard. Isn't she stunning? She's going to be a model," Karen reported. Her big hazel eyes danced as she added, "I'm so glad me and Diana and Vi are in social studies and math together and so is Cass Johns."

Karen recited these names with a lilt in her voice, then paused, waiting for me to list *my* new friends, too. I said, "I've got a lab partner."

"The girl I saw you with at lunch today?" But Munch didn't even wait for my nod before rushing on, "Listen, I'm not taking the bus. Kenny's driving us to Diana's house."

"Who's Kenny?" I asked, and she said with pretended nonchalance, oh, one of Diana's friends, who was a junior and just *happened* to own a totally cool car.

Munch's mother was so strict that she wouldn't even let Karen watch TV on weeknights. Mrs. Tierney made Karen account for every minute she spent out of school. "She didn't say you could go?" I gasped, and Munch gave me an "are you kidding?" look.

"I called Moms at work and told her I was going to granny-sit with you. Okay, ol' pal, ol' buddy?"

I started to tell her never mind the ol' buddy stuff, then looked down at the hand she'd laid persuasively on my arm. Karen's nails had been chewed down to the quick, and there were little, red, half-moon marks all over her hand. When she got really down about things, Munch chewed on herself.

"Things bad at home?" I asked sympathetically.

"Same old, same old. Moms is driving me nuts. Like she's afraid that if she leaves me alone, I'll turn out to be ba-ad, like Daddy, so she watches me like she's the CIA or something."

Karen paused. "Sometimes I'm tempted to *be* rotten, Megs," she added bitterly. "Just to show her she was right about me being sinful. So, will you cover for me, or what?"

What could I say? Not liking it, I nodded anyway, and Munch gave me a hug. She then commenced to tell me more about her new friends, and the cute boys ("I mean, they're *upperclassmen*, Megs—sophomores and *ju-niors*, even! Imagine that, and we're just dorky little freshmen. I mean, I am, not Diana and Vi and Cass.") that hung around them. It was typical Karenspeak—she was always flip and funny and liked to talk a mile a minute—but today I could feel the nervous tension that edged her words.

I didn't like this tension. It reminded me about the bad vibes at home. Vibes like, would Mimi be confused when I got home this afternoon? Like, would Mom call sometime around five and say, could I please have dinner alone with Mimi because she wasn't able to leave the store. And like the jumpy feeling that hung around us even when we *did* have dinner all together, the brooding, waiting silence that made my stomach curl with acid and the food taste like cotton wool.

Worst of all there was the memory of what had happened yesterday, and Mom saying that they'd talk about Mimi *later*, in a way that made me hope later would never come.

"It was a mistake to bring her to live with us. She should have taken that apartment at the Heathers two years ago when your father died."

It was close on ten o'clock, and my folks had just gotten home from the store. I'd been studying in my

20

room when I heard them arrive and had come down to say hi, but now I wished I'd stayed upstairs as, pausing halfway down the stairs, I watched Dad pacing the den floor.

Mom had plopped down into an overstuffed armchair. Her back was to the light, and I could pick out the tufts of gray in her curly, fair hair. Her voice was weary as she said, "We all decided at the time that she was better off with us than at a retirement community. Mama was all *right* then, Jerry, so don't start blaming me at this late date."

Her usually gentle voice was irritable. Dad stopped pacing and rubbed a big hand over his face, spreading the furrow between his eyes and massaging his receding hairline.

"Why do you always say I'm blaming you? You make me sound like the bad guy, and I'm not." Then, tiredly: "I've always liked your mother—you know that. But we just can't watch her twenty-four hours a day. Regina Cruss isn't reliable, and we can't afford a full-time companion for her."

"I could—"

"Quit work and take care of your mother yourself? Nolly, we've been through that. If we don't make a success of Naturfoods, we're up the proverbial creek."

Breaking off, Dad headed for the kitchen to pour coffee. "You'll get acid in your stomach," Mom warned automatically.

"Call Sidwell Home and Meadowriver again. Call all the places where she's on the waiting list. Maybe somebody's died, and—Meg, is that you on the stairs?"

I hated feeling guilty when I'd done nothing wrong. "When did you start eavesdropping?" Dad demanded.

21

His harsh voice scraped against something raw inside me. I wasn't used to, didn't *like* having my father snap at me like this, but lately it seemed that was all he did. I could hear the defensiveness in my voice as I told him I'd just come down to say hello.

"I didn't think you were telling secrets," I added.

Dad turned away. Mom said, "Meg, there's a real problem. After yesterday, we feel that Grandma can't be left alone anymore."

"She could've been hurt walking all the way to Six Corners. She's a danger to herself," Dad added wearily.

"You're not going to put her in a—a *home*?"

Mom said nervously, "Keep your voice down, Meg, she might hear you. Anyway," she went on, "the long-term-care facilities we saw are very nice. Meadowriver, especially. It has an atrium, and a baby grand piano in the recreational room, and all kinds of programs and outings. I saw cloth tablecloths and real flowers on the tables in the dining room, and the staff is so nice—even Mama said they were nice. Right, Jerry?"

Mom sounded like she was talking about a new summer camp. "Why does she have to go to a—long-term-care facility, anyway?" I argued. "She was fine today. We had a good time at dinner, and she ate well, and everything." No answer. "She'll *hate* it," I added fiercely.

Dad slammed down his coffee cup, stalked to the window, and leaned both hands against the sill. "What would *you* suggest? You want to quit school and stay with her all day, is that it?"

Anger cut a sharp ridge in his voice. The muscles in his neck stood out in tense cords. Mom eyed him uneasily and said in a fake-cheerful tone, "Speaking of school, Meg, how is it going? With all that's been going

22

on, I didn't even ask you how your first day at school was. Right, Jerry?"

A moment's pause, and then Dad nodded. "Yes," he said. Trying to sound enthusiastic and involved, he added, "Tell us about the big new high school."

He swung away from the window, strode over to sit down in the chair next to Mom's, and they both looked at me: she, tall and plump, soft and fair; he, dark, smaller, compact, and as tightly wound as the insides of a golf ball. It was like, okay, Meg. Tell us something that'll make us forget this thing with Mimi.

It was up to me, so I tried. I told them that South Regional was humongous with an enrollment of about two thousand kids. "None of my friends from eighth grade are in any of my classes," I added. "I don't see Karen one time during the whole school day."

"You'll make new friends." Dad yawned, excused himself. "Anyway, you and Karen talk on the phone every night. The filibuster twins."

For a second he sounded almost like my old, wise-cracking, fun-to-be-around father. But Dad's words also brought home the fact that Munch hadn't called me today. Whenever I'd phoned *her,* her line had been busy.

Munch had new friends to talk to, whereas I had only one. "Well, sort of a friend," I amended. "Rea Alvarez. Ms. Llord assigned us to be lab partners."

Just then there was this snorting sound from Dad. "He's gone fast asleep," Mom whispered. "It's been a rough day. Tell us more about school tomorrow, okay?"

As I nodded I had the feeling that my folks weren't

really interested in school, anyway. Well, get real, Meg, how could they be interested in school stuff with everything that was going on with Mimi, and the store—

"Mom—is Naturfoods in trouble?" I asked.

Her soft lips quivered uneasily. "It's all right," she said in a way that made me sure it wasn't. "A new business takes at least a year to turn over, honey. Things are a little difficult till then." She sighed. "That new health-food store at Six Corners hasn't helped, either."

The folks' franchise, into which they'd poured about every cent they had, was located in the Wellford Mall, two towns to the east of us. It was an older mall, and the huge, modern health-food store at Six Corners was doing a number on their business.

"I could help at the store after school," I offered.

"Thanks, baby, but no. You have to study, okay? Dad and I decided when we started out in business for ourselves that no matter what, we weren't going to do anything that would interfere with your schooling." A pause. "Besides, there's Mimi. Somebody's got to stay with her."

Mom broke off, slid out a deep breath that was almost a sigh. "Sometimes I wonder if we didn't rush into the franchise too quickly, but then I remind myself that it's a sound business. As your father says, it'll take off given time." She looked at Dad beside her, head bent down on his chest. "We just need time," she repeated.

Mom didn't sound too convinced, and even asleep Dad looked worried and unhappy. "I know it hasn't been easy for you, either, Meg," my mother was going on. "We'll just have to do the best we can, okay?"

She spoke cheerfully. But as I went upstairs I saw her

24

lie back into her chair and cover her eyes with both hands in a way that brought a hard knot into my throat.

The life that I'd known and loved was changing, too. Blowing, blowing away.

THREE

Next day when Ms. Llord handed back our homework, mine had a huge, red *Incomplete* printed across the page. *This is a warning,* Ms. Llord had written. *From now on, anything less than your best will result in an F. I expect this to be redone. Neatly,* in *ink and on my desk by tomorrow morning before homeroom.*

My day proceeded to get worse. After biology, Mr. Jacobs whacked us with a sneak quiz. That, plus all the work that was piling up for Ms. Llord, destroyed what little appetite I had, and I gloomed down to lunch, where Karen came bouncing over to me.

"Come on over and sit with us," she said. "I've saved you a seat."

Munch nodded to a table where three girls were already seated. I hesitated because just then I'd spotted Rea sitting alone at a table at the far end of the cafeteria. She had her back turned toward us.

Karen saw me looking. "Is she waiting for you?" she asked. "Did you tell her you'd sit with her?"

"No," I said, "but we had lunch together yesterday."

"Soo? You have to sit with a lot of new kids or you'll never meet anyone. Come *on*." Karen gave my arm a persuasive tug. "Don't you want to sit with us?"

Feeling a small twinge of guilt, I followed Karen to her table. I kept glancing over my shoulder to see if Rea was looking for me or waiting for me, but she didn't once look my way. Meanwhile Karen was bubbling, "Guys, this is my friend Meg Fairling."

They all looked me over, and the one called Diana said, "Hi, Meg. I'm Diana."

Diana's eyes were a clear green, and both her eyebrows and her long eyelashes were a shade darker than her red-gold hair. She had, I noted, a nice smile.

"Cass Johns," Karen proclaimed, waving at a tiny, doll-pretty blonde who looked as if she'd walked off the set of *Annie*. "And this is Vi Rochard."

Today the towhead was wearing an oversized peach silk blouse over slouchy, string-tied pants that looked like pjs. Still managing to look elegant, she gave me a long, assessing stare before nodding. The tiny blonde waggled her fingers in cheery greeting. Diana said, "Hi. Karen says you guys have been friends for all your lives, practically."

"That's really fat," Cass approved, when I nodded. Diana said that it was so cool and sounded as if she meant it.

"The only person I've known since grade school is a real dork," Vi contributed. She drawled her words, and her hazel eyes declared that Munch's and my history was totally boring.

"We've been best friends forever, right, Megs?" Karen said eagerly. "We used to hang together since first grade. Sleep-overs and cookouts and all that stuff. We used to—"

"We get the picture," Vi drawled.

"I think it's so excellent to have old friends," Diana said as Karen flushed and dried up. "My parents moved

27

to Chisolm while I was in fifth grade. All because of my dad's job. So instead of old friends, I get these characters here."

She gestured to Vi and Cass, who chorused, thanks a lot, Diana. "Her father's the CEO for Lartheon Electronics," Karen enthused. "He's the *man,* Megs."

"C'mon, don't make it sound like such a big deal." Diana smiled. "I'm sorry you and Karen don't have any classes together, Meg."

I warmed to Diana, liking her more and more. Cass seemed nice, too, though I wasn't at all sure about Vi, who drawled, "I wish *I* could move and leave my dumb parents. I'm sick of them using me like a yo-yo while they're sticking pins into each other."

Cass and Diana nodded sympathetically. I glanced at Karen, who mouthed "divorce" and then pretended to look at something else when Vi caught her at it.

"You don't have to whisper," the towhead said. "It's no big deal. My ever-loving parents have been talking divorce since I was practically an infant. They just can't make up their frigging minds."

All I could think of to say was, "So, did you three guys all meet each other in middle school?"

"Good old Chisolm Middle School—" Vi broke off suddenly. "Well, *look* who's here, girls."

We all followed the direction of Vi's gaze. Surely, she couldn't mean— "I thought Rea Alvarez would be in jail by now," Vi drawled.

"What are you talking about?" I demanded. "What's wrong with Rea?"

"You *know* her?" Cass chirped. I explained that we were lab partners in Ms. Llord's class, and Munch's new

28

friends exchanged looks. "Oh," Cass then went. "So it's not like you're friends or anything, then. That's a relief."

Vi was still staring at Rea's back in a way that made me feel really uncomfortable. "Why shouldn't I be friends with Rea?" I asked. Once more, a knowing look flashed among the three.

"She's bad news," Vi said, stretching each word as long as she could. "Really, really, baaad news."

I glanced over my shoulder again at Rea, who was eating steadily, her eyes pinned on a book she'd opened beside her tray. "She's nice, and she's really smart in biology," I protested. Looking at Vi defiantly, I added, "I *like* her."

"Oh boy," Cass murmured. "*Oh* boy. Maybe we should tell her, Diana—"

"No," Diana said firmly. "We promised not to talk about *that*. Let's just change the subject, okay?"

Vi rolled her eyes. Cass shrugged. I persisted: "What's Rea supposed to have done?"

"There's no 'supposed' about it. We actually watched her—"

"Shut up, Vi," Diana urged.

She sounded upset. Cass added in her breathy little voice, "Like my mom says, if you've nothing really fat to say about somebody, it's better not to say anything at all."

"Give me a *break*." Vi folded her arms across her chest as she added, "She's a criminal, that's all."

"Vi!" Diana said, really angry now. "Cut it out. Just stop it right now."

"You want Meg to get in trouble?" Vi swung sharp hazel eyes toward me. "*I* think she should know that Alvarez's father's in jail for murder."

I admit to feeling a second's chill. In that instant I remembered how, during all our talk yesterday, Rea had never once mentioned her father. "So what?" I argued. "What does that have to do with Rea? *She* didn't do anything wrong."

For the third time Diana, Vi, and Cass looked at each other. "You tell her," Cass chirruped. "You do it, Diana."

Diana said reluctantly, "This is all confidential, okay? The truth is that—well, Rea's a thief."

Rea? Stunned, I stared at her tense back and suddenly recalled the way my lab partner had stiffened up yesterday when she had seen Karen and her new friends in the cafeteria. "I don't believe it," I stammered.

"We saw her shoplifting, Meg. Last spring we were downtown shopping at Creeden's in Six Corners—you know the variety store?" I nodded. "Well, that day we saw Rea there," Diana went on. "We knew her from school, so we were walking over to say hi. Then, when we were a few yards away from her, we saw her put a bracelet in her pocket."

"We weren't the only ones who caught her," Vi continued. "The store manager grabbed her and marched her back into his office. I guess he called the police."

"We got out of there quick in case they asked us if we'd seen her do it," Cass added. "We didn't want to, you know, snitch on her."

Rea had gotten up and was carrying her tray to the counter. She didn't look our way, but I knew she'd seen me. I felt I should walk over there and say hi, but I didn't.

Rea, a *thief*? I just couldn't picture her as a thief. "We were, you know, in shock," Cass was saying. "Like Diana says, we knew her from school. She always seemed an okay person to me."

"Except for that perfume," Vi snitted. "Wheeew."

Angered by her cattiness, I persisted, "Like I said, we have biology lab together. She's really smart."

"Maybe—" Diana stopped, shook her head. "No way am I going to tell you what to do, Meg."

"What Diana means is that maybe you shouldn't get too friendly with Rea." Cass leaned across the table to whisper, "I heard she's into drugs and stuff."

Drugs. The lunch I'd just eaten clumped into something hard and cold in the pit of my stomach. "Have you seen her do drugs?" I asked Cass.

"Sure we have," Vi cut in. "So will a lot of people real soon." Diana shot her a hard look. "Well, people who are hooked on drugs get careless, don't they?"

"And you get pegged by who you hang with," little Cass added.

Now all of them were watching me. I felt as if I should defend Rea, but I couldn't think of anything to say. And Karen, who'd been looking from one to another of her new friends in surprise, made it worse.

"Poor Megs," she went. "The one person you get close to at South Regional has sticky fingers."

Which was Munch's totally tactless way of summing up a real problem. I'd figured Rea to be a shy loner, but what I'd just heard explained *why* she was alone. *If* what I'd heard was true. Like a hurtful bur, that thought clung to me for the rest of the school day and it followed me out to my first meeting with the girls' track-and-cross-country coach, a lean, mean individual named Mr. Prudhomme.

According to him, we were no longer in the baby farm of middle school. "To be included in the South Regional Freshmen Girls Cross-Country Team is an honor you've

31

got to earn," he informed us. Then he added that after a week the useless among us would be winnowed out.

Winnowing with a vengeance, he ordered us freshmen to run high knees—"Get those knees *up,* girls, don't let me catch you jogging on the straightaway!"—and repeated quarter miles till we were ready to throw up. Then, rusty ferret eyes contemptuous, he asked us if we thought we were athletes or maybe just wusses in running shorts.

I'd figured I was in pretty good shape, having run all summer, but by the time Mr. Prudhomme'd finished with us, I could barely limp home. There I found Mimi taking a nap, so I went to my room and started on my homework. Or, *tried* to start, because I found that instead of concentrating on Ms. Llord's assignment, I kept thinking of Rea and what the girls had said about her. Rea, a shoplifter. Rea, a convicted murderer's daughter. Rea, a druggie—

The phone rang on my bedside table, startling me so much that I dropped my biology notebook. "I'm sorry, honey," Mom's voice said apologetically, "but we're going to be working late. Can you fix yourselves something and we'll grab a bite out. Okay?"

This made it the fourth time this week that Mimi and I'd been left on our own, but apparently it couldn't be helped. A new shipment of goods had come in that afternoon, and they all had to be on the shelves and ready for sale for tomorrow.

"How's your grandmother?" Mom then asked. I started to tell her that Mimi was napping, whereupon she cut me off in midsentence. "I've got to go. *Counting* on you, Meg, okay?"

I fixed Mimi's favorite dish—liver and onions—and

called her down to eat. She'd woken up from her nap in a quiet, faraway mood and ate mechanically, her eyes on her plate. I tried to get a conversation going, but Mimi didn't seem to hear a word I said.

Used to this, I slipped into a familiar game. I told Mimi what Diana Angeli had told me about Rea, then asked and answered questions to myself.

"Should I ask Rea if what the girls said was true?" I asked. "You think I should, huh? I don't know much about Rea Alvarez, but she really seems nice. The thing is, Diana's really nice, too. I'm sure she wouldn't say anything that wasn't true—"

"There are two roads leading to the truth," Mimi said suddenly.

I was so surprised that I blinked at her. "Then I should ask Rea what happened at Creeden's?"

But Mimi just looked confused and asked, what was I talking about? and I pushed down the knot in my stomach and told myself never mind. At least Mimi knew who *I* was, I comforted myself, so that was okay. Hey, who cared about short-term memory, anyway?

Besides, Mimi'd given me the answer to my question.

Next day I got to biology class early, and the second Rea came through the door, I went over to her. "I'm sorry about not having lunch with you yesterday," I began.

Rea shrugged. "It's okay. I know about these old grade-school friends, eh? So, how does Karen like South Regional?"

In spite of her carefully casual tone, I sensed that she was uneasy. Her discomfort infected me, and I said much too heartily, "That Munch—she's already friends with half the school. I met some of her new friends yesterday—

Diana, Cass, and Vi. I guess all you guys were in Chisolm Middle School together."

Rea didn't say anything, but something in her body language changed. "So, *were* you friends?" I prodded.

"Is that what they told you?" she came right back, and all at once it didn't seem like such a good idea to ask her anything more.

As I started back to my desk Rea went, "I want to hear what lies Diana Angeli told you about me." I told her, never mind, let's forget it, but she wouldn't let it go. "No," she said, "you *tell* me what she said."

Reluctantly, really sorry now that I'd begun this, I mentioned the shoplifting and saw the anger flash in Rea's dark eyes. Then the anger dulled away, and without a word she started to arrange her books on her desk. "Rea, it's not true, is it?" I demanded.

She wouldn't look at me. "If I say it's a lie, you wouldn't believe me." Her voice shifted to almost a whisper and I had to strain to hear her add, "Looks like an angel, but inside, she's a devil."

Just then, Ms. Llord walked in and called us to order. As I took my seat I glanced over at Rea again, saw that she was chewing her lower lip and that her hands were shaking.

"Rea," I whispered, "listen, I'm not saying I *believe* them, okay? I just—"

"No talking," Ms. Llord decreed, but for once I was so upset about Rea that I hardly cared what Lord Doom might do to me.

"If it's not true, you should stand up for yourself," I urged.

"*Meg!* One more word, and you have detention *with me*!"

34

I shut up, but I watched Rea's tense profile. I wished I'd never said anything, wished she'd write me a note or even glance my way. She didn't. All through the long period she just stared at her desk, and I felt as if something hard had wedged itself in my throat. I didn't know what to think. I mean, if someone had told lies about *me,* boy, I'd sure have defended myself. Whereas Rea had said nothing. *Nothing.*

When the period ended I tried one more time. Running after her, I caught her in the corridor near my locker. "Look," I said, "maybe I shouldn't have said anything, but if it was me, I'd want to know what people were saying so's I could set things straight. I mean—"

"Just leave me alone!" Rea snapped. Then she took off down the hall. As she went she muttered something else that seemed more to herself than aimed at me. I wasn't sure, but I *thought* she said, "What's the use?"

When I got home after my second day of tryouts for the cross-country team, I found Mimi in the garden. She was whistling a tune from one of her favorite Rodgers and Hammerstein musicals while she weeded the chrysanthemum patch.

"Where's Mrs. Cruss?" I asked.

"She had to take her granddaughter to the pediatrician again, so I told her I would try and stay out of trouble while she was gone." Mimi pushed back her old straw hat to regard me with a slightly crooked smile. "Are things all right in your neighborhood?"

She was herself today. Relief did funny things to my insides as I said, "Yeah, sa' right."

"But?" Mimi glanced up from the chrysanthemums

35

and I caught a flash of amethyst eyes. "The running's not going well?"

How many times, I wondered as I plopped down beside the chrysanthemums and felt the sun-warmed grass tickle my legs through my jeans, how often had I come to Mimi for advice? Long years ago, when I was a little kid; later, when my folks were both working and I'd stayed at Mimi and Papa's after school.

Talks at her piano while our twenty fingers flew in duet, heart-to-hearts at bedtime, and now, here, in this September garden with Mimi wiping her gloved hands on her dungarees. "So, what's troubling you?" she was asking.

"Not what. Who. Rea Alvarez is my lab partner in biology." Mimi nodded. "I hear she's a shoplifter."

Mimi pulled out a weed and laid it gently on the pile of weeds beside her. "How did you 'hear' this?" she asked.

"Through one of Karen's new friends." I explained about Diana, Cass, and Vi. "I guess they were in Creeden's—you know the variety store at Six Corners—and they saw Rea shoplift. I asked Rea about it, but she didn't deny it. She didn't say anything at all."

" *'Qui s'excuse s'accuse.'* " Mimi rocked back on her heels and gave me this thoughtful look as she translated, " 'He who excuses himself accuses himself.' Or, perhaps she was too hurt to reply."

"I wish I hadn't said anything." I sighed.

"You did what you thought was right." Mimi took off her straw hat, mopped her forehead, then touched a large white chrysanthemum as gently as she touched the keys of a piano. "This beautiful flower only lives a short time. I keep trying to tell Nolly and Jerry how important time is, but they ignore me and keep working like ants. That's not right."

"They have to work to make the shop successful," I defended my folks. "There's a lot of competition from the health-food store at Six Corners."

"They're at the shop every day until nine. Sometimes ten." Mimi shook her head. "They should have kept their old jobs."

Dad had quit his store manager's position at Save and Shop to buy the Naturfoods franchise. Mom had left her bookkeeper's job at Lartheon Electronics. That was where Diana's father was the CEO, I remembered.

"And to think they sank all their funds into ginkgo tea and ginseng jelly," Mimi went on sadly. "Tofu in the ice cream, for heaven's sakes, and alfalfa pills. It's enough to give a hippopotamus indigestion."

Listening to her, I started to grin—but then remembered my problem with Rea. "What should I do?" I asked. "Talk to Rea again?"

Mimi dug in the dirt around one of the chrysanthemums, then tamped it smooth. "Who's Rea?" she asked.

Okay, it was always happening, I should be used to it by now, but I felt awful as I gathered myself up and went into the house. I went upstairs, threw my books on the bed, and flung myself after them, so that Gorki, who'd been snoozing on my pillow, opened both eyes and stared at me.

"It sucks," I told her bitterly.

The phone rang, and Karen's voice bubbled at me from the other end. "Hey, hey," she said. "You took like *forever* to get out of practice. Are there any cute boys running with you, or what?"

Karen knew very well that the boys had their own

37

team and their own cross-country coach. Unlike Prud-homme, the boys' coach was a really nice guy. In fact, I knew Mr. Hargen personally, since he lived a couple of miles down the road from us.

Playing Karen's game, I said, "There's a cute guy from biology class who's a runner, too, name of Jed Berringer."

"How cute? No—never mind. He's probably tall and weedy with running shoes and a number on his back." Munch paused. "Listen, Diana wanted me to call and ask you if you want to go with us for ice cream at Six Corners. Moms isn't here, so I'm going to take off before she comes in and tells me I can't go. Want to come?"

It sounded like fun, and while I was with the girls I could maybe ask more about Rea, too. Tempted and hopeful, I looked out of the window to where Mimi was still gardening, but there was no sign of Mrs. Cruss's car in her driveway. "I can't." I sighed.

"Oh, yeah—I forgot. Your grandma, huh? It's too bad, but there'll be other times." She paused. "I'm glad the girls like you, Megs."

"You mean they don't think I'm like Rea?" I couldn't help asking.

"Well, there's a reason they don't like *her*," Munch reproved. "You sound stretched, Megs. You need to loosen *up*."

I thought of Rea's suddenly shuttered face and her tense silence. "Rea Alvarez sounds like a loser to me," Karen was rattling blithely on. "A dad in jail and all that shoplifting stuff. Megs, you don't mind that I'm leaving a note telling Moms I'm studying over your house? If she calls you, tell her I'm there."

So that was the real reason she'd called. I tried telling

38

Munch I didn't like being used as an alibi, but she did the old Karenspeak thing, talking so fast I couldn't get a word in edgewise. "Don't you *love* Diana? And Cass is nice, too—the boys are all crazy about her. Vi—I mean, she's snotty sometimes, but that's because she's having a hard time with her *parents*. I love her clothes and the way she does her eyes. And, Megs, I mean, her parents are the pits, always sticking the knife in each other and trying to get Vi to side with them and stuff. Listening to her tell about it, I'm *glad* Moms divorced Daddy."

After some time of this she hung up. I'd hardly put the receiver back in the cradle when Mom phoned from the store. "Let me guess," I said. "You're not going to make it home to dinner."

Mom didn't tell me not to be so flip. Instead she sighed and said how sorry she was. "You don't know how I wish I could be home for one dinner with the entire family."

Well, Mom, I nearly told her, I wish you could, too. She made it sound so easy: fix a casserole, Meg, have dinner with Mimi, you don't mind do you, baby? But suppose I *did* mind? Suppose, just for once, that I'd wanted to go have ice cream with Munch. What about that?

Downstairs, Mimi had begun to play something by Liszt. Listening to that shadowed music, I felt even more depressed. I loved Mimi, truly, truly loved her, but sometimes—

"Sometimes I need time of my own," I told the dead phone angrily. Sometimes I needed to get away from worrying about school and from worrying about Mimi. Sometimes I wanted to just have a good time and hang out with my friends—

Friends. Once more Rea's face came swimming up in front of my mind's eye.

39

Okay, I thought. Okay, I'll talk to her again tomorrow. Maybe Rea'd figured I was accusing her, and that had made her mad at me. She probably was totally innocent. And even if she wasn't, people made mistakes, right? I knew for sure that I had. Tomorrow I'd tell her so, and we could start all over again.

But biology was sixth period on Fridays, which meant I had to get through almost the entire day before I could talk to Rea. I kept looking for her in the corridor during passing, but there was no sign of her. And there was no sign of her at lunch, either.

Karen was there, though, sitting with Diana, who at once waved me over. Then, while I was going through the line, I saw Vi and two guys join Munch and Diana. One of the boys was a hunky, macho-type dude with short brown hair, a lifter's shoulders and thick neck. The other was tall, thin, and nervous looking.

"How's your day been, Meg?" Diana asked as I came up with my tray. "How's Ms. Llord?"

"If you have Lord Doom, your day just has to be bad," the thin boy announced. He then commenced to pound two fingers, drumlike, on the table.

"Meg, this is Kenny," Diana explained. "He had Ms. Llord last year." She nodded to Macho Man. "And this is B.K."

B.K. barely grunted, but the one called Kenny told me, "I had Llord two years ago, when I was in ninth grade. That old witch and me came close to war."

He had quit drumming his fingers and was now flipping his spoon up and catching it again. "Sure—and I bet you won the war, right?" B.K. jeered. "You talk too much, Draper. That's how come you got an F from her."

Kenny snorted. "Nobody wins over that old battle-ax,"

40

B.K. went on. "She's been with this lame school for like a hundred years, and even MacMasters is scared of her."

"One time when I was in her class, Ma went in to see her." Kenny tossed his spoon high, caught it again. "Ma starts out by saying she doesn't know much about biology and Lord Doom gives her one of *those* looks and goes, 'Then it's a good thing you're not in my class.' Ma nearly took a fit."

Everybody at the table laughed. Diana said, "See, you're not the only one with problems, Meg."

"And the poor girl has *serious* problems," Vi announced. She began to play with one of the dangling, silver moon earrings she wore. "Meg's got Rea Alvarez as a lab partner."

The boys looked at each other, and Kenny started laughing. "No fooling," he yelped. "So tell me, is lab the only thing you girls do together?"

He broke off and commenced coughing so hard that he had to pull some kind of spray out of his pocket and zot himself a mouthful. Meanwhile Diana directed him to leave me alone. "Meg is our friend," she added.

Over Kenny's coughs, B.K. said, "Alvarez sure gets around." I guess I looked bewildered. "She's a party girl," he explained. "A slut."

Idly, Vi continued to play with her earring. "We didn't tell you yesterday, Meg, but your pal Rea's involved in more than the sticky-fingers department. She likes to sleep around."

I felt as if somebody'd hit me in the stomach. "I don't believe it," I heard myself say.

"Show her," Vi directed Kenny, who, still coughing, groped around in his jeans pocket and pulled out a folded sheet of paper, which he shoved across the table at me.

41

"Take a look," he wheezed.

I unfolded the paper and nearly gagged. There was a picture of Rea sprawled out on a bed. The photo was kind of smudged from having been run off on a copying machine, but it showed that Rea was naked except for black bikini underpants. Underneath the photo was written, *For a good time, call me,* followed by her name and phone number.

"This dorkhead actually called her," B.K. said, nodding at the gasping Kenny. "Called her and asked her for a date."

Kenny took another snort of whatever was in the spray, shrugged, and gave a thumbs-up sign with both hands. "I believe in free enterprise," he went. "It's the American way."

"She'd be too much for you, boy," B.K. kidded. "Your asthma'd have gone into hyperdrive and you'd have dropped dead."

Kenny said it might have been worth it. Diana said she didn't want to hear that kind of talk. "But what did she *say*?" Karen wanted to know. She seemed fascinated by the smudged flyer on the table.

"She hung up on me, but I figured she wasn't *alone*." Kenny began to tap out a fast tempo on the edge of his lunch tray. "I mean, she's not a bad-looking chick if she didn't use that lame perfume. She may have other, ah, clients."

With hands that were shaking, I grabbed the paper, crumpled it up, and drowned it in my mashed potatoes. "Hey, why'd you do that?" Kenny spluttered. "That was *mine*."

My voice was shaking worse than my hands. "It's

42

sick," I exclaimed. "I don't believe she—I just don't believe it."

"Grow up, Meg, this is high school, the big leagues," Vi drawled impatiently. "I mean, why did Alvarez shoplift? She has a habit to support, that's why." Then, seeing that I didn't get it, she laid it out for me. "Drugs, dummy. Rea's a druggie."

Wanting to repeat that I didn't believe her, I held back. Suddenly I wasn't sure *what* I should believe.

"You don't know Rea very well," Karen said uncertainly. She looked at me and it was like, Please don't keep arguing with my new friends, Megs.

"Well I don't blame Meg—that flyer is disgusting," Diana defended me.

"It sure *is* gross," Karen agreed promptly. "Taking a photograph like that and—and circulating it to the boys in school. She's a tramp."

Vi rolled her eyes as if to say, What did I tell you? Diana just said, "Let's talk about something else. What are we going to do this weekend?"

Just then, Cass came into the lunch room. As she came trotting over with her tray Vi drawled, "You took your time."

"It *takes* time to do things right," Cass protested.

She and Diana nodded at each other. Then she turned and sent B.K. a glance that practically sizzled the air. "I'm *sorry* I'm late," she purred.

B.K. got a little red, grinned, and dragged his chair closer to Cass's. As the two tuned into each other, plans for the weekend started again. And while they talked I kept thinking of Rea. Not about the Rea pictured on that horrible flyer but the girl who'd talked about her little sisters and about her grandma and about becoming a teacher one day.

"It doesn't make sense," I muttered.

Diana looked at me questioningly, but I didn't push it. Didn't say anything more in Rea's defense. What *did* I really know about her, anyway? Not much. And I was beginning to think that maybe there were a lot of things about my lab partner that I didn't want to know.

FOUR

BACK IN FIFTH-PERIOD study, I thought about it. And the more I thought, the more I knew I didn't want to get involved. Mimi was enough for any two people to worry about. Besides, Rea had made it plain she wanted no part of me—

My thoughts tailed off into the wailing of a police siren that seemed to be coming straight at us. "Someone's getting busted," one of the kids shouted. He ran to the window, calling, "Hey, check this out—they've got the canine patrol here, too!"

Ignoring our study aide, who screeched that we were to Be Silent and Sit Down, we all crowded around the window. A squad car was parked in front of the school, and a van marked K-9 DIVISION had driven up behind it. As we watched, an officer led a big German shepherd down from the van, and they both began moving purposefully toward the school.

Just then the buzzer went. Grabbing our books, we all dashed outside. A small crowd had gathered near the three-hundred-wing lockers, and we headed toward them.

Jed Berringer was one of the crowd. "What's going on?" I asked him.

Before Jed could answer, the double doors at the end of

the three-hundred wing parted and the officer with the German shepherd came walking through. A second policeman, walking just behind him, was talking to Mr. MacMasters, who looked grim enough to drink battery acid. Bringing up the rear was Mr. Gorland, the janitor.

"Somebody called the school and said that drugs were stashed in the three-hundred wing." Cass was standing next to me, her books clasped to her chest, her face intent. "I had to get a late pass at the office," she went on, "and I heard Mr. MacMasters calling the police."

We all watched the officer walking his furry partner up and down the rows of lockers. "Ooh, is he going to *my* locker?" a nasal voice wondered.

Cass rolled her eyes. "Doris Leo, the freshman dork," she declared. Then, glancing at me, she went, "I know, I know—that wasn't nice to say. But Doris is in English with Diana and me, and she, like, is such a know-it-all." She paused. "Lookit—the dog's found something."

There was a collective gasp as the policeman pointed to one of the lockers. "Can we have this one opened?" he asked our principal.

Mr. Gorland stepped forward and opened the locker. There was a collective sigh as the officer reached in and withdrew a small plastic bag and opened it. "Marijuana," he said. "Whose locker is this?"

"I never put that bag into my locker!"

I cringed to hear that familiar voice. Beside me Cass murmured, "Rea Alvarez."

Now do you believe me? her tone of voice implied. I was too shocked to say anything, could only stare at Rea, who looked wild-eyed and scared as MacMasters barked, "What do you mean, it's not yours? Isn't this your locker?"

46

"It's my locker, but I d-didn't put that bag inside." Rea was so nervous she was stammering. "I never saw that bag b-before."

"Any idea how it got into your locker, then?" Mac-Masters glared at Rea, then at the rest of us standing around. "In my office," he snapped at her, then commanded, "The rest of you—back to class."

As we all scattered to our classes, I turned back to look at Rea. She seemed so small, walking down the corridor between MacMasters and the policeman who held the brown paper bag.

"It's crazy." Jed had fallen into step beside me. I glanced up at him, and he went, "Rea goes to my church. I'd swear she doesn't do drugs."

Rea and drugs. Rea featured in that awful flyer that Kenny had shown me—and here was Darryl Haas waiting for us in the doorway of biology class, his face alight with malicious pleasure.

"You heard about Alvarez?" he chortled. "The cops found grass in her locker. She'll be suspended for ten days, that's the rule in this stupid school."

I glared at Darryl, but he just winked at me as he followed Jed and me into the classroom. "They'll take Alvarez down to the police station and charge her with possession. She'll have to go to court. *Bus-ted!*"

"Give it a rest," Jed interrupted. Darryl demanded, why should he, and Jed snapped, "*I* say so, okay? Just keep your mouth shut."

"Yeah?" Darryl pushed his broad face close to Jed's. "You going to make me, or what? Huh? What're you going to do?"

Looking straight in Darryl's piggy eyes, Jed said, "For starters, I'm getting a new lab partner."

47

I couldn't help laughing at the look on Darryl's face—he knew he'd fail the labs without Jed's help. He cut me an evil look, but Ms. Llord's appearance sent him sulking to his seat. Class began. No one dared breathe a word about what had just happened, but Rea's empty desk was an awful reminder.

Karen had all the news waiting for me when she met me by my locker after school. "Can you *believe* it?" she chattered, after she'd informed me that Rea'd been taken away to the Chisolm police station, where she'd been booked for possession. "I mean, I knew you really didn't believe Diana when she said all that about Rea."

I started to say something, then paused to give Munch a hard look. "What have you done to your eyebrows?" I demanded.

"Oh, this?" Karen tried to look casual. "Vi plucked them for me during study. You have to, you know, pluck the eyebrows to open the area around the eye. How do I look?"

Opening the eye area had given Munch a startled, almost rabbitlike look. Hedging, I said she looked different. "Different is good," Munch then went. "Vi says—oh no, Megs, isn't that Ms. Llord calling you over?"

Lord Doom was standing in the doorway of her classroom and beckoning. I looked around in the hope that she might be paging someone else, but nobody else was around, so I had to go.

I was racking my brains wondering what I'd done wrong when she handed me a set of papers trapped in a notebook. "These are for Rea," she said. I stared at her in bewilderment. "Here is her laboratory notebook and instructions for tomorrow's lab," she explained. "And this

48

is the material we covered in today's lesson. I want you to take these to her."

She was kidding, right? No, wrong—Ms. Llord's ice-blue eyes were dead serious. "But," I protested, "I have tryouts. Besides, I don't know where Rea lives."

"She lives here in Chisolm at one-oh-eight Filbert Street," Ms. Llord informed me. "Here is her address and a copy of the map of Chisolm. I understand you ride your bicycle into school most days, so you can deliver the homework after you run."

I protested, "There are other kids in the class who live right here in town. I—I have to get back home right after tryouts. And anyway, it'll be late. Maybe her folks could swing by the school and pick this up."

"Mrs. Alvarez works very hard all day," Ms. Llord said, and I remembered what I'd heard about Rea's father. "You are Rea's lab partner and so the logical choice," she continued crisply. "She requires her home-work, including updates on the lab work, each day, or she will fall behind."

I should have asked her to make a switch earlier, I thought dismally. Meanwhile Ms. Llord was saying, "Please inform her that you'll be bringing her assign-ments to her every day."

She turned back to her desk, sat down, and began to correct a paper. Discussion over. "Ms. Llord, Rea had drugs in her locker—"

"I heard what went on this afternoon. Rea has been *ac-cused* of drug possession and is possibly in violation of the substance-abuse policy. But accusation is not proof of wrongdoing."

Ms. Llord aimed those last two sentences over my head, and I realized that Mr. MacMasters was standing in the doorway. He frowned at Ms. Llord and rasped out, "According to the policy of the school, suspended students may not make up their classwork."

"It has always been *my* policy that students should be given the opportunity to keep abreast of *my* class," Ms. Llord came right back. "The student is more important than policy to me, Mr. MacMasters."

Sure that our principal would blast Ms. Llord to the ground, I was totally shocked to hear him sigh. Then, without another word, he walked away.

As if nothing had happened, Ms. Llord continued to correct papers. "Please inform Rea that you will pick up her homework on Monday when you deliver the next assignment," she instructed me.

Mumbling a reply, I booked it into the corridor, where Karen was waiting for me. When I told her what Ms. Llord had commanded me to do, she almost sputtered with indignation.

"Who does she think she is, ordering you around? You should have told her you wouldn't do it."

Which, I said, proved she didn't know Ms. Llord. "Even MacMasters doesn't want to argue with her," I pointed out. "And you think *I* can?"

Two hours later, knees aching from Mr. Prudhomme's torture, I was riding my bike through Chisolm with Ms. Llord's map in my jeans' pocket. Luckily, Filbert Street wasn't hard to find.

An older section of town, it lay parallel to Main Street. Here the houses were set close together and built on postage-stamp lots. Some of the houses had chipped paint and a few of them looked like they needed repair. Quite a few of them, though, had gardens that Mimi would have approved of, and there was the happy sound of kids playing on gym sets and in sandboxes.

The Alvarez house had the peeled-paint look, a front porch cluttered with bicycles and toys, and a yard made cheerful by spunky chrysanthemums and marigolds. As I got off the bike a dog, Heinz 57 and ancient, raised his head and gave me a long, patient look.

"Hey, guy, howar'ya," I said.

The dog got carefully to his feet and stiff-legged it over to me. He rubbed his nose in my jeans, got interested in smells of Gorki, then apparently found me acceptable and lay down again. I went up onto the porch and pressed the doorbell.

Nothing happened. Maybe the bell wasn't working? I knocked on the wooden door, and after a while I heard footsteps approaching. Then Rea opened the door.

"What do you want?" she demanded.

She was wearing a baggy old Red Sox sweatshirt and a pair of scruffy jeans. She had a bottle of spray cleaner in her hand as if she'd just been doing housework. She looked like any kid I knew, not someone who'd been kicked out of school for stashing drugs in her school locker.

"Ms. Llord sent your homework," I said.

There was a flicker in her black eyes. She opened the door a crack wider, and now I heard a burst of little kids' laughter from within. "You came all this way to bring me my homework?" Rea wanted to know. I held out the book and the sandwiched papers, and she added, "Thanks. Do you want to, you know, come in?"

There was a plea in her voice. She wanted me to come in, talk to her, say I didn't believe that she was a druggie or a bad person. I knew that. But just now I was tired and

51

sore from Prudhomme's torture, and the memory of that disgusting flyer made me feel so uncomfortable in Rea's presence that I wanted to get away as fast as I could.

So I deliberately pretended to misunderstand her and said, "Hey, you're so smart, you'll know what has to be done without my explaining it to you."

The light in her eyes flicked out. Wordless, she took the homework from me. As she did so her lab notebook slipped and fell to the floor. A sheet of paper fell out, and to my total horror, I saw that it was another one of the flyers with her nude picture on it.

Rea made this strangled noise in her throat. She grabbed the flyer and tore it into a billion pieces. Then she glared at me. "You, too?" she cried.

"Look, I didn't even know it was there—" But it was too late. She'd slammed the door in my face.

Saturday morning I slept in. Lying in bed I could hear my folks talking downstairs, getting ready to—what else?—go to the store. Saturday was a busy day for them. I could hear my dad's deep voice raised in argument and my mom's softer one replying. Familiar sounds—but even in my drowsy condition I knew that something was missing.

Mom had used to laugh a lot. She had a lovely laugh that started deep in the stomach and then exploded into high notes. Hearing Mom laugh, you couldn't help feeling good, and Dad would often tell her crazy jokes just to get her started.

Nowadays Mom hardly laughed anymore, and Dad seldom cracked a smile, let alone a joke. I burrowed my head in the pillow to escape that thought and was falling asleep again when the doorbell rang. A few minutes later

Mom was at my door. "Meg," she went, "wake up." I mumbled a protest and she added, "The police are here. They want to talk to you."

The *who*? I raised my face from the pillow, saw that Mom was looking bewildered but not really scared. "Has—is Mimi okay?" I blurted.

"What?" Mom looked even more distracted. "Your grandmother's still asleep. The policewoman said that they want to ask you some questions about a classmate."

I felt a twinge of irritation. Rea Alvarez, of course—who else? I wished that she'd never been in my biology class and that Ms. Llord had never made us lab partners.

Cass was right; you were judged by the people you hung around with. I wondered if the police had seen me taking Rea her homework and figured I was doing drugs, too—

By the time I'd thought this, we'd reached the stairs. Peering down, I saw Dad talking to two uniformed police officers: a short guy with graying hair, and a heavyset woman with hair slicked back from her face.

They both looked up when I came down, and the woman said, "Hi. I'm Officer Oakes and this is Officer Denton. We're with the Chisolm Police Department. Are you Meg?" I nodded warily. "We want to ask you some questions," Officer Oakes went on in a friendly voice. "How well do you know Rea Alvarez?"

"We're lab partners in biology," I mumbled.

"But you went to see her at her home yesterday?"

"I took her homework to her." I looked from one officer to the other. "Ms. Llord told me to."

"Oh, yeah, Ms. Llord," Officer Oakes said, and grinned. "I had her, too, when I went to SR. So what time did you go to the Alvarez house, Meg?" I told her. "Did Rea seem upset or disturbed in any way?"

"What's all this about?" Dad interrupted. He was rocking back and forth on his heels, his short, compact body tight with the frustration of not being able to get going. I could hear him thinking that he should've left for the store fifteen minutes ago. He opened in twenty minutes.

"Rea Alvarez was found dead this morning," Officer Denton said. He had a small, soft, almost apologetic voice. "She apparently hanged herself in the night. Her mother found her this morning."

My stomach felt like it had fallen a thousand feet. "She's—no way, she's not *d-dead*?" I stammered.

Both cops nodded. Mom said, "Oh my God." Dad also did a double take, then frowned and asked what this had to do with his daughter. "According to our information," Officer Oakes answered, "Meg was the last one outside the family to see Rea alive."

My stomach flooded with bile. I wanted to throw up, but my legs wouldn't work to take me to the bathroom, so I sat down on the bottom step of the stairs and clasped my arms around my middle, holding back the nausea while Mom whispered, "*Why?* Why would a young girl kill herself?"

"We're trying to find out, ma'am." Officer Oakes turned back to me. "Meg, you didn't answer my question. Did Rea sound upset to you? Different in any way?"

Sure, she'd been upset, I wanted to shout. They'd found drugs in her locker, she'd been suspended, for Pete's sakes. And then there was that flyer— "We've seen the flyer," Officer Denton said when I began to stammer an explanation. "We know about the suspension. Is there anything else you can tell us? Do you know any of Rea's other friends? Her mother seemed to feel that there were some students at school who hated Rea and wanted to hurt her."

Should I tell the police officers what Karen's friends had said about Rea? But none of the girls had wanted to hurt her, and besides, what good would it do to rake up more bad stuff now that Rea was dead?

No good—and it might get Diana and the others in trouble. So I just said that I hadn't known Rea very well. "She went to Chisolm Middle School before coming to SR, so she'd have known the kids from Chisolm better."

Apparently satisfied, the officers went away. Mom shut the door after them and then stood there with her hand on the knob for a long moment until Dad asked, "Are you okay, Nolly?"

"I'm thinking of that poor mother, finding her daughter like that," Mom said in a low voice. "It's so tragic. So sad. What would drive a young person to kill herself in such a terrible way, Jerry?"

Dad massaged his face as he always did when he was upset. "You heard what the police said—she was in trouble and didn't know how to handle it. Maybe she had problems at home. Maybe she was just lonely—"

He broke off and said that he was sorry, but he had to go; it was past time to open the store. Mom looked uncertain. "Mrs. Cruss promised that she'd come by to spend some time with Mama this morning. What do you think, Meg? You and I could have lunch, just the two of us, and talk—"

Yes, I wanted to shout. But then I glanced at Dad, saw from his expression that he was hoping I'd refuse Mom's offer. "It's up to you," I mumbled, "but I'm okay."

"Well . . ." My mother actually looked relieved, and I

felt a sudden stab of unhappiness. *She*'d been hoping I'd say no, too.

Saying that they'd try and get back early tonight, my parents left. I went upstairs to take a shower and all the while I stood under the hot water I thought of the way Mom hadn't really wanted to spend time with me. I thought about Rea and her shy smile that did *not* match up with the drugs in her locker or that nude photo of her. And around the edges of those memories I saw again the hopeful look Rea'd given me when I'd handed her the biology homework.

After my shower I went downstairs and poured myself juice. Big mistake. As the sweet liquid went down my throat I thought of how Rea's throat must have been burned as she knotted the rope and put it around her neck.

"I didn't do anything to you," I muttered. "You did it to yourself, okay? You should blame yourself, not me."

" '*Et tu, Brute?*' "

Mimi's voice behind me nearly made me drop the glass of juice. I must have jumped a foot. "Scared you, huh?" Mimi asked.

She looked frail and brittle in her aqua robe, but she was smiling in her old way, and the warmth of that smile made me blurt out what was in my mind. "Rea Alvarez killed herself."

Mimi looked puzzled. "Do I know her?"

I went over the whole story, and Mimi listened carefully. "That's too bad," she said at the end of my recital. "Poor young girl, to have been so hopeless. But then, things always seem more hopeless when you're young. When I lost my first boyfriend back in high school, I thought my heart would break."

56

She tapped her chest. "Guess it didn't," I said.

"No. But sometimes young people can't cope with what's happening. They opt out of the pain, taking a permanent solution to a temporary problem." Mimi went to the refrigerator and poured herself some juice with a steady hand. "I'm sorry for your friend, Meg."

"She wasn't really—" But I stopped because Rea was dead and saying I hadn't been her friend seemed too cruel, somehow. We'd had lunch together one time and talked about our grandmothers. We'd done a lab together. I'd taken her her homework one time, and she'd slammed the door in my face.

"Do you know what made her despair so?" Mimi wondered. She put toast in the toaster, made a choice between strawberry and marmalade, carried all to the breakfast nook. She moved with grace and assurance and strength, and I let myself relax. For now, my grandmother was okay.

Abuelita gave me this.

I shut my mind to Rea touching the cross at her throat (her poor, bruised throat!) and told Mimi about the drug raid. And because this was Mimi to whom I could tell everything, I explained about the disgusting flyer that Kenny had shown me.

"Cruel," Mimi murmured. "Children can be so cruel."

Shaking her head, she began to eat her toast. I started telling Mimi about my taking Rea's homework to her and resenting it, but I didn't. I was too ashamed to admit even to Mimi that I'd cut Rea off when she'd wanted a friend.

"When is the funeral?" Mimi suddenly asked. I said I didn't know. "You'd best find out, hadn't you?"

"Mimi," I protested, "I didn't really know her. She was my lab partner, not really a friend."

My grandmother considered this for such a long time that I thought she'd forgotten what we were talking about. I was surprised when she said, "But from what you say, she knew you and liked you. Go to the funeral, Meg. Funerals are for memories. Memories are the only way we living can hold on to those we love."

I sure hadn't loved Rea, and I no way wanted to hold on to any part of her. But rather than argue the point, I asked Mimi if she wanted a piece of the sports page, which of course she did since it had an article about the Patriots in it. And then, while she was reading it, I thought of Rea again.

Go *away,* I told my memories silently. Go away, Rea, and leave me alone. I hoped Mrs. Cruss would come soon so that I could take off—but to where? I phoned Munch, and her mother told me Karen was studying in the library. "I thought you were going to meet her there, Meg," she added.

Mrs. Tierney made everything she said sound like an accusation. I said that I'd gotten a late start, thinking, all the while, that Karen had to be with Diana and the others. And she hadn't even bothered to tell me about it.

Loneliness filled me, then rolled wavelike away, leaving me feeling empty. I would have liked to beat it to my room, but Mrs. Cruss was just now plodding up the driveway. As Mimi went to let her in, the phone rang.

"Hey, hey," Karen sang, "what's going on, Megs?"

Munch's voice sounded strange, as if she were standing in a wind tunnel. "Oh, that's because I'm using the conference phone," she said airily. "Diana's got one at her house."

She then proceeded to tell me that everyone was there—Cass, Vi, and Kenny. "We're just dishing about stuff and listening to tunes," she reported happily, "but we're leaving soon because B.K.'s playing in a game with West Braden High. Kenny's driving us to watch, and then we're going to go blading."

"Want to come, Meg?" Diana's equally tinny-sounding voice asked. "It'll be fun."

I could hear laughter and talking in the background. The sound of it teased without filling the emptiness inside me. "I can't," I said.

"Don't tell me you need to granny-sit again. You really need to get a *life*." Karen sighed. Then, without missing a beat, she added, "Did you hear about Rea, you know, killing herself?"

I told her that the police had been here, and now everybody got into the act. What did the cops want? Vi wanted to know and Cass chirruped, "What could they want from *you*?"

I explained about the biology assignment. "Whoa"— Munch sighed—"better you than me, Megs. Moms would have taken a fit if I was friendly with some crazed druggy." A pause. "I guess Rea couldn't live with herself anymore."

"Why should you bother to guess?" Vi snorted. "She was doing drugs, she was stealing, she was selling her body, and she got busted. It all hit her at once and she couldn't think of any other way out."

Maybe that was true, but Vi's unsympathetic drawl grated on me. Somewhere in the background I could hear Kenny urging the girls to get going before they missed the first half, and that bugged me, too. "Did you tell the cops what we told you about the shoplifting and stuff?" Vi was asking.

I said no. "That was nice of you," Diana said. She

sounded sad. "I mean, she's gone. Why say bad things about the dead?"

Kenny yelled that he was leaving. Cass chirped that they had to *go* or they'd miss B.K.'s game. Karen bubbled excitedly. "I'm sorry you can't come, but I'll catch you later, Megs, 'kay?"

Last night Rea Alvarez had fitted a noose around her neck and ended her life, and here my best friend was worrying about being on time to some ditsy football game. Rea Alvarez was dead, and Vi brushed her off as if she hadn't mattered. Rea'd been so desperate that she'd hanged herself, and there wasn't even a ripple in the pool that showed she'd ever been alive.

It wasn't okay, I wanted to tell Karen. It wasn't *okay* at all.

FIVE

MONDAY, SCHOOL WAS buzzing with the news of Rea's suicide and kids were disbelieving and scared. One girl started crying in homeroom and had to be sent down to the nurse.

I went to biology feeling miserable and hoping that, under the circumstances, Ms. Llord would go easy on us today. Instead of which she announced that we were going to have lab and that the results of our lab work on cell membranes were going to count as a quiz grade.

"In this lab we will look at the different properties of the cell membrane," she intoned, "while manipulating another lipid bilayer—soap. You'll learn some facts about a dynamic and complex structure."

What was she talking about? But before I could look up *bilayer* in my notes, she added, "I see that Darryl is absent. Meg, you and Jed will work together."

As we set up I warned Jed that I was totally clueless. "You can't be worse than Darryl," he reassured me. "Cells are interesting stuff. You'll catch on."

Jed's MO was different from Rea's. Where she'd been swift and sure, he worked with a careful, almost loving deliberation that made it easy to follow and understand. As we mixed liquid soap with warm water, added teaspoons of Karo syrup, and mixed gently ("Carefully, careful, we can't let the bubbles break"), he hummed under his breath.

Following Jed's lead, I made a bubble holder out of straws and string and managed to get a soap film on it. "Lookit, if you put this pen through the soapy film, it won't pop—it's self-sealing," Jed explained. "That's just like a cell membrane. There's a membrane around each of the billions of cells in your body, each of them self-sealing."

I was actually becoming interested in what was going on when he suddenly asked, "Are you going to Rea's funeral?"

The unexpected question caught me off guard. "I don't know," I stammered. "Is it today?"

Jed shook his head. "Saturday at St. Martin's Catholic Church," he told me. "The old one, not the new one with the modern roof. It's right on Mountain Road."

I knew which church he meant. I'd run or biked by it often enough. But why the delay? I asked Jed, and he said he'd heard that there'd been an autopsy, and besides that, the family had wanted to wait until her aunt, who'd had minor surgery in Puerto Rico, was well enough to travel.

Before he could say any more, Ms. Llord decreed that we were now to detail our findings so that we could discuss them as a class. For the first time I was grateful to Ms. Llord. She'd saved me from giving Jed an answer about going to Rea's funeral.

The truth was that I didn't want to go. I'd only been to one other funeral in my life—my grandfather's—and even with the whole family with me, it had been a grim experience. I didn't know Rea's family. I hadn't really known *her*.

The guidance counselor came to talk to us during social studies, and we discussed Rea's death and what it meant to us. After that, it was natural to talk about the funeral. There were kids in the class from Chisolm Middle School, but they hadn't been friendly with Rea. Others didn't even know her and said they'd feel weird going to the funeral, and Doris Leo—the one Cass had called the freshman dork—insisted that going to the funeral of somebody you didn't even know was disrespectful. "We'd be, you know, like rubberneckers at a traffic accident," she added.

Doris was a big girl with a loud voice and a sinus condition that made her sound nasal all the time. She hadn't been popular in middle school because, as Cass had pointed out, she always acted as if she knew it all. But this time, I had to admit, she had a point.

Rea's death made everything else seem unimportant. Even the fact that I'd actually made the cross-country team didn't seem to matter. But the reality that I was now a member of "Prudhomme's Squad" showed up in the fact that I soon became one massive ache.

Prudhomme's schedule had us racing each Thursday. This meant that Monday was endurance day—seven miles up rocks, tree stumps, and hills, with Prudhomme shouting for us to pump those arms, keep our eyes *up,* and to take bigger strides, what was the matter with us? On Tuesday, lest we get soft and wimpy, we had "hard training" day, which I grew to loathe worse than a toothache.

From this torture I would crawl home and fall asleep over Ms. Llord's homework. At night I dreamed of Mr.

Prudhomme yelling, "Focus, girls! Go faster, you're not trying hard enough! You think you'll ever make it to Springfield if you run like a lame duck?"

The Springfield state meet was apparently Prudhomme's idea of heaven. In November, at the end of the season, after the league meet and the Class-A meet, the best runners statewide would gather together to compete at this event. Prudhomme told us that in years gone by a few of his runners had made it to Springfield. "Not that I see anyone of that caliber *this* year," he added, "though a few of you might be decent runners if you put your minds to it."

With my crazy new schedule, I hardly had time to talk to Karen. My first race on Thursday had come and gone before our paths finally crossed on Friday. When I got to lunch on Friday, she bounced up from her table and waved me over to join her and the others, who were all ranking on the pizza.

"Cardboard," Vi was commenting disdainfully as I came up with my tray. "Def-i-nite-ly cardboard."

"Hey, want to come over to my place tomorrow afternoon and try making some real pizza?" Diana asked. There was a chorus of agreement. "How about you, Meg? Can you come? Kenny'll pick you and Karen up. Right, Kenny?"

The thin boy nodded in time to the drumbeat his fingers made on the table. "I'm the best pizza delivery-man there is," Kenny joked, and got pink in the face when Diana smiled at him.

"So, can you come?" Munch urged.

"I think so," I said, and she beamed, glad that I'd finally, officially, been included in the circle of these wonderful new friends.

"We'll have fun," she enthused. "Diana's house is so *phat*."

Cass's favorite word on Karen's lips seemed out of place. I tackled my pizza, which definitely was like cardboard, and listened to the talk ebb and swell around me until Diana said, "You're awful quiet today, Meg. Problems with your grandmother?" I asked, should there be? "Well, I heard she gets confused sometimes, you know, like the time that she went and played the piano at that music store," Diana explained.

I glanced at Karen, who avoided my eye. What had given her the right to gossip about Mimi? I felt myself go all bristly until Diana reached out and gave my shoulder a little squeeze. "I didn't mean to make you feel bad," she said gently. "I know how you feel. My gramps was the same way a few years before he died. He was the sweetest old guy."

At the sadness in her voice, my defensiveness slid away. "Did he live with you, too?" I asked.

"In our house?" Diana looked almost shocked. "Gramps? Not that he wouldn't have wanted to, but my mother would never have let him clutter up—I mean, it just wouldn't have worked out."

She gave me a long, thoughtful look. "I bet you and your grandmother are real close." I nodded. "I envy you, you know? Gramps was a sweetheart, but the nursing facility he lived in was like an hour's drive away, and my folks were really too busy to visit him much."

As I listened, I thought of what Rea had said about her old grandmother. Would Diana understand how close Rea'd been to her *abuelita*? I half opened my mouth to tell her but stopped. It was Rea's grandmother and her

65

story. It didn't seem right talking about it now that she was gone.

"Everybody's got a problem, right?" Diana was musing. "There's Vi's parents doing the on-again, off-again marriage thing that drives Vi nuts, and then there's Karen who can't breathe without her mother wanting to know what for. And then there's Kenny—"

"What about me?" Kenny wanted to know. He dropped a couple of spoons he'd been juggling. "What're you saying about me, Diana?"

"That you're a doll," she said. She put a hand on Kenny's arm and patted it gently. "You are, you know. If we didn't have your wheels, we'd never get to *do* anything."

Kenny was so pleased that he flushed all over, choked, and started to cough. "Watch it, you'll get the poor fool so excited he'll have an asthma attack," B.K. kidded. He slipped an arm around Cass. "Then we'll have to take Draper's pizza to the hospital."

Vi snickered. "We could, you know, make a pizza for Alvarez, too. You know, like the ad says, put it on her Tombstone."

There was this silence into which B.K. snorted uneasy laughter. Karen looked uncertain. Diana said sternly, "Vi, that wasn't funny."

"What's the matter with you?" Vi demanded. Under carefully applied makeup, her cheeks glowed with sudden, angry color. "Why are you acting so holy? You're the one who said—"

"Shut *up*, Vi!" Diana exclaimed sharply. "You aren't being funny, okay?"

Vi got up, picked up her tray, and stalked off. Diana

66

watched her go with an exasperated expression in her eyes.

"I don't know what gets into that girl." She sighed. "She's having a tough time at home, but that's no excuse to joke about Rea's death like that. Poor kid—I heard the funeral is tomorrow, but I don't know anybody who's going."

"Not me." Kenny coughed, and the others shook their heads. As I watched them, I had this sickening feeling of déjà vu. This same table not long ago, these same people ranking on Rea, and me sitting here quiet, not sure enough of myself to speak up in her defense. Now the world had turned around and come back to me again.

"I'm going to the funeral," I said. Then, as they all stared at me, I added, "She *was* my lab partner."

So, just like that, I'd decided on doing what I'd never figured I'd do. I thought Karen might call to talk me out of going to Rea's funeral, but the phone didn't ring once that evening. So next morning I came down to breakfast in my white blouse and good black slacks, and Mom offered to take time off from the store to drive me to St. Martin's.

I said thanks, but it was okay, I'd take my bike. "But what about your friend's pizza party?" Mom wanted to know. I told her that Karen and I would be going together. "I can pick you girls up," Mom then offered. "I'd like to meet your friends."

But I knew she'd get busy at the store and hate to leave Dad shorthanded—or worse, she might forget to show. So I said don't worry, I'd be fine.

It was a cool, gray morning and there was a head wind to battle as I pedaled down Mountain Road. This long, sometimes lonely, often narrow road wound its way into Chisolm and brought me right to the old-fashioned Catholic church with a statue of the Virgin Mary in front.

Inside St. Martin's there was a scent of wax candles, incense, and flowers, and a closed coffin with a spray of white chrysanthemums across the lid. Looking quickly away from that, I saw stained-glass windows and a huge cross with Jesus suffering on it, and statues of the saints. There were a lot of people inside the church, and a pew marked with white flowers in front where the mourners were going to sit.

Jed Berringer was sitting alone on a pew near the back. I slid in next to him. "I don't see anybody from school here," I whispered.

"Some of the kids from middle school are here—and her." Jed nodded to a pew two rows ahead of us.

Ms. Llord wore a dark suit and a matching dark hat. She sat straight with both feet firmly on the ground and hands folded over the pocketbook in her lap. She was listening to a lady seated beside her, a blond lady with Jed's lean face and strong bones.

Jed made a face. "That's my mom. Can you believe it? A funeral, and she's getting a private conference."

As he spoke two ladies came trudging down the aisle, knelt, crossed themselves, and slid into the pew between us and Ms. Llord. The rounder one was shaking her head and the thin lady in the hat with feathers was sighing and saying, poor girl, oh, that poor girl.

"Such a shock," the fatter lady agreed. "And then, all that trouble about the funeral ceremony. Father Valera's from the old school, so old-fashioned! It nearly killed Arianna when he said that though he'd perform the service, she had to realize that as a suicide Rea could never enter paradise."

I cut a shocked glance at Jed, who shrugged and whispered that it was old-fashioned thinking. "How could the priest tell that to Rea's mother?" I argued. "It's awful."

Jed's reply was drowned out by the deep, mournful notes of the church organ. As the music rose a Hispanic man came out of a side door. His hair was cropped short, and he had a little mustache, and he was dressed in a shirt and tie. His hands were folded in front of him, and his suit jacket was draped over the wrists. Two men walked on either side of him.

Right away the ladies in front of us commenced nodding and shaking their heads. "They let George out of prison to come to his daughter's funeral," the fat lady said loudly enough to be heard over the organ sounds. "Imagine. Having to come here to this house of God with two guards. Having to go back to MCI Cedar Junction after that poor child is buried."

The skinny lady craned her neck to get a good look. "He must feel so guilty," she hissed. "If he hadn't gotten drunk and knifed that man he worked with, it'd have been different for the whole family."

She was about to say more, but just then Ms. Llord turned her head and fixed both ladies with an icy look that totally shut them down. I glanced at Jed to see if he'd caught Lord Doom at work, but he was watching Mr. Alvarez and his guards being seated just behind the mourner's pew.

Now an elderly priest led out the mourners. First came an old, heavyset lady, veiled and dressed totally in black. She was leaning on a younger woman. Behind them, flanked by two little girls, came a lady who looked as if she were sleepwalking. "Mrs. Alvarez," Jed whispered to me.

Rea's mother was covered from head to foot in black. A black veil shrouded her face, but something in the way she moved made me think of Rea and the way she'd looked at me that last time I saw her.

That spooky thought kept me company as the ceremony started, with the priest talking about Rea as a dutiful daughter and a loving sister, a good niece and a devoted grandchild. Rea would take her grandmother for walks. She minded her siblings while her mother worked. She was a good student who worked hard at school.

As he spoke the old grandmother rocked back and forth and began to wail. That seemed the signal for everyone in the mourning party to start crying. The little kids sobbed and wiped their eyes with their sleeves. The aunt moaned. Mrs. Alvarez buried her face in her hands and you could see her whole body shuddering with her sobs.

Other people in the church were crying, too, saying the Rosary and crossing themselves. "That poor Arianna," the woman in front of me told her companion. "Rea was her right arm."

Finally, the service was over. As we stood up for the mourners to walk past us down the aisle and out of the church, I asked Jed if we had to go to the graveside. "I'm not really up to that part of it," I added, and he said neither was he. "Now explain that stuff about Rea not getting into heaven," I went on.

Jed said that anybody who died in mortal sin supposedly went to hell. "A suicide dies in mortal sin," he then said.

"So she's supposed to be in hell now?" I demanded.

"Well, maybe she's in limbo—that's a sort of a place between heaven and hell." Jed paused. "Hey, that's not what *I* believe, but our priest's real old-fashioned, and he plays it by the book."

As he spoke the mourners slowly walked up the aisle. Everyone was weeping, and the old grandmother was crying noisily and talking in Spanish. As she passed I heard her say, *"Ay, santísima, santísima, qué malo es el ángel."*

"How evil is the angel—probably blaming the evil angel—you know, the devil—for tempting Rea to kill herself," Jed translated somberly.

The old lady was still talking, her voice rising shrilly over the silence. "C'mon, Mama," the woman with her said, and taking her arm, began to lead her away from us. "Come, *mamacita,* let's go home now."

But one member of the mourning party couldn't go home. I glanced over my shoulder and saw that Mr. and Mrs. Alvarez were hugging each other as best as they could given his handcuffs. For a moment they clung together, and then Mr. Alvarez's guards led him out of the side door. As Mrs. Alvarez watched her husband go, I saw her shoulders slump in total despair.

Rea would stay in limbo for eternity and her father had to go back to prison. "You know what?" I told Jed angrily. "This whole thing totally sucks."

As I spoke Ms. Llord came walking up the aisle with Mrs. Berringer. She caught my words, turned, and gave me one of her pale, ice-blue looks.

"It most certainly does," she agreed.

When I got home, I found a black Pontiac Firebird, its decal spread-eagled across the hood in red and yellow, parked by the door. Inside, I found Kenny and Karen sitting in the den with Mimi.

Kenny was tossing a pillow from one nervous hand to the other while describing some kind of football play. "You're exactly right," Mimi was saying as I walked in. "He should have opted for the lateral pass. That mistake cost him the game."

Kenny nodded eagerly and went on talking. He hardly noticed my arrival, but Karen ran over to me demanding, "Where've you *been*?"

I said I was sorry to make them wait, that I'd change and be down in a minute. Praying that Mimi wouldn't fade out in the middle of her conversation with Kenny, I went upstairs, and Karen trailed after me.

"Poor Kenny," she went. "If it wasn't for his asthma, he'd be one of the jocks. He *loooves* football." She paused to glance pointedly at her wristwatch. "I don't understand why you went to the funeral, anyway."

"You should have gone on ahead to Diana's," I said.

"Oh, come on, lighten *up,* Megs." Karen hopped on my bed and bounced a little. "Was the funeral really bad?" Then, before I could answer, she went, "Megs, wear that shirt *over* your jeans. Looks fat that way, y'know?"

Another fashion tip courtesy of Vi? Noting that Munch today wore an oversized silk shirt on top of what looked like pj bottoms, I defiantly tucked my shirt in and said I was ready to go. "Mrs. Cruss's walking over to the house right now," I said.

Downstairs, Ken and Mimi were still talking football. I kissed my grandmother good-bye, and she patted my cheek. "You young people have fun now. And, Kenny, I'll bet I'm right about Sunday's game."

"Your grandma sure knows a lot about football," Kenny said as we followed him to the car. He sounded impressed.

So Mimi hadn't disgraced me in front of my friends. A little ashamed of the relief I felt, I explained that my grandmother had been a die-hard Patriots fan since day one. Kenny looked even more respectful. "I wish *my* grandma was like her." He sighed.

Karen sat up in front with Kenny, I sat in the back. Kenny talked football all the way through town and into Chisolm. Letting Karen handle the small talk, I slid my mind back to the funeral this morning. I thought of what the ladies in front of us had said and of Mrs. Alvarez's ravaged face.

"It's not right," I muttered.

"That's just what I said—it's the pits. But refs are born blind," Kenny agreed heatedly.

As he spoke we pulled into a street that was lined with trees. The houses, set far back from the road and surrounded by more trees, were huge, and the Angeli house was the largest of them all.

Karen turned around to smile blithely at me. "Isn't it *phat*?" she caroled.

Phat wasn't the word. At a front door that looked as if it had cost more than our entire house, Diana was waiting. "Hey, you guys," she called, "we were beginning to wonder if Kenny got stopped for speeding or something."

Kenny and Karen both pointed to me. "It was my fault," I admitted. "I'm sorry."

"Well, don't stand there, come on *in*." Diana held the door wide-open, and we walked into a hall that was all white—white tiles, white walls, skylights through which

73

white sunlight filtered. The walls were covered with art-work that looked like someone's doodles but that had to be megaexpensive.

The hall led us past a humongous living room with a huge marble fireplace. Over the fireplace was a bigger-than-life oil portrait of a slender woman with Diana's red-gold hair and dark eyebrows. She was dressed in what looked to be white and silver gauze and had this sil-ver band with a crescent moon on it circling her fore-head. In her hands she held a silver bow and arrow.

"That's my mother," Diana explained casually. "She's dressed as Diana the Huntress."

"You look like her," I said.

"Yeah—so they say." Was I imagining a sudden dry note in Diana's voice? I glanced at her, but she was smil-ing as she went on. "The story is that my mother and fa-ther were dressing up for Mardi Gras, and Pops took one look at her as Diana and said, 'I want a portrait of you just like that.' "

"You were named after a goddess, right, Diana?" Eyes wide with hero worship, Karen repeated, "Diana, the Huntress."

"Are you guys going to take all day?" B.K. had stuck his head out of a room way down the hall. "I'm ready to die from hunger."

Diana laughed. "Come on," she told us, and we trailed after her to—I kid you not—a totally *white* kitchen. Not only were all the cabinets, floors, ceilings, and utilities white, but so were the fixtures. White shades, scrolled with silver thread, softened the light at the floor-to-ceiling win-dows. Music from hidden speakers engulfed the room with Aerosmith.

"Hey, look who got here, finally," Vi drawled from the

74

depths of a white wicker chair. "About time, too. B.K.'s been on a liquid diet."

B.K. raised a beer can to us and shook it gently. Cass, who was sitting cross-legged on the floor by the window, chirped, "What took you so long? Was the funeral *that* interesting?"

Kenny headed over to the spotless white refrigerator, opened the door, and pulled out a beer and began chugging on it. Vi watched me through eyes she had outlined with green to match the emerald tee she'd tucked into snug white pants. "So, how was it?" she drawled.

"It was just a funeral," I said, wishing they'd leave it alone.

"Well, she's buried and it's over." Kenny downed his beer and looked moodily at the can. "And I'll never know how much fun she could be in bed."

Kenny began to juggle some hot pads. "Drugs and sex and rock and roll," B.K. said, "plus a little shoplifting thrown in. She was one wild and crazy broad. Too much for you, junior."

He lifted Cass up and sank with her into another wicker chair. Perched on B.K.'s lap, Cass persisted, "Were there many kids from school?" I said, only a few—plus Ms. Llord. "Not Lord Doom—oh, *phat*!" Cass exclaimed eagerly. "Was her father there? Sometimes they let criminals out of jail for funerals."

"He was there," I said. Since they were all listening, I went on. "And it wasn't fun or anything, believe me, it was pretty grim. Mrs. Alvarez looked really rough. And the grandmother kept crying and saying things."

Vi, who'd been studying her nails—painted green, too, I noted—suddenly lifted her head. "What did she say?" she wanted to know.

75

I said that she'd mostly spoken in Spanish. Diana looked somber. "I wish now I'd gone to the funeral, but I really didn't know Rea at all. Maybe one day I'll take some flowers to her grave, may she rest in peace."

"I'd rather rest in pizza," Kenny said, and Vi yawned and said that she was totally grossed out by this talk of funerals and could she eat, please?

Diana opened the refrigerator and started to take out bowls and jars. "Everything you need to create, cook, and devour your own custom-made pizza," she announced.

As she said, there was everything a pizza cook would need. Dough. Sauce. Veggies and sausages, pepperoni and salami, and all kinds of cheese. Diana pointed us to pizza-pie plates, handed out spotless aprons, and pointed to where we could wash our hands. "Hand towels are here," she said.

Everything had its place. "Isn't this a really fat kitchen?" Karen asked me as I started to roll out my dough. "It makes ours look sick."

"It's excellent," I said, but actually I wasn't so sure if I meant it. At home, I'd have tossed stuff on my pizza and had fun doing it, but the Angeli kitchen was so sparkly clean and orderly that it made me a little nervous. But I was apparently the only one to feel this way, because the other kids were busy creating their pizzas. Kenny, especially, was dumping everything but the kitchen sink on his masterpiece.

"Lookit," Cass chirruped. "B.K.'s building a skyscraper."

Peppers, onions, mushrooms made the first tier, and then cheese, and pepperoni and scads of salami, and more cheese. "Hey," B.K. said, "I only put the best food there is into this body."

76

"Too much beer already went into that body," Cass murmured. She patted his lean belly, and B.K. laughed and turned around to grab her. As he did so his elbow caught a big glass jar of pizza sauce. It fell to the floor and broke.

B.K. swore. Kenny laughed. Diana said, "It's not funny. You made a terrible mess!"

She ran across the kitchen, grabbed some paper towels, and began mopping up the mess on the floor. Just then a husky voice exclaimed, "Well—I hope you're enjoying yourselves."

A woman had walked into the room, and for a second I thought that it was another Diana. Then I realized that though she was as slender as Diana, this woman was older, taller, and wore her strawberry-blond hair cut short to the ears. Her pale peach blouse exactly matched her slacks and she carried a peach sweater slung casually over her shoulder.

"Hi, Mrs. Angeli," Cass and Vi chorused.

Mrs. Angeli smiled at them. "I'm not staying to ruin your party, Diana. I'm on my way to—" She broke off as her eyes went to the mess on the floor, and her smile died.

"I was just going to clean it up," Diana said quickly. "It was an accident."

"I knocked the jar over," B.K. apologized.

"If the jar had been in its right place, accidents wouldn't happen." Mrs. Angeli's voice had gone cold, and her eyes, a paler green than Diana's, were icy. Her lips were thin, as if they'd had practice folding into a disapproving line. "You know how I feel about messes in my kitchen, Diana. I've told you many times that I won't tolerate dirt."

"I said I'm going to clean it *up*," Diana said through her teeth. She tore off a wad of paper towels and got down on her hands and knees.

A frown furrowing her brow, Mrs. Angeli watched Diana mopping up the mess. "Make sure that you get rid of the paper towels properly," she directed. "They will attract vermin."

Nobody said anything. Without looking at anyone, Mrs. Angeli walked out of the kitchen. As we heard her heels tapping down the hallway, Diana rocked back on her heels and exhaled deeply. "Count to twenty, real slow," Cass advised. "It helps."

B.K. said awkwardly, "Look, it was my fault."

As if she hated them, Diana tore another handful of paper towels off the roll and mopped up the remaining mess. "My mother is always obsessing about things," she muttered. "Everything has to be in its place, everything has to be scrubbed spotless, everything has to be the way she wants. She drives me *nuts*."

I thought of our kitchen, which Mom was always complaining was too small. The last time we'd baked cookies, it had looked like a tornado'd hit it. There'd been cookie dough smudged all over the counter and on the floor, and a bag of chocolate chips had lain open so we could all sneak a few, and there'd been flour on Mom's nose. I thought of the warm baking smells, of the coffee Mom and Mimi brewed to drink while waiting for the next batch to come out of the oven, and the laughter.

How long ago had it been since we'd had fun like that? I couldn't remember. To shut down the stab of loneliness churned up by that memory, I knelt down on the floor and started to help Diana. "No," she snarled, "stop, you fool. You're doing it wrong."

78

Taken aback, I looked up and saw that her eyes were dark with anger. Pupils dilated, face pale, she glared at me as if she hated me. For a second I didn't even recognize Diana.

"Cool it, Angeli," Vi drawled.

She looks like an angel, but inside, she's a devil—
Qué malo es el ángel.

Rea's muttered words, her grandmother's keening voice, both hit me from left field. That evil angel, Rea's *abuelita* had said. But surely she had meant the devil, Satan, the evil one?

Diana was still fuming. "My damned, compulsive mother. God forbid that anybody or anything should mess up her precious house or her clothes, or her life. Everything has to be done her way. Sometimes I wish I could tell her to go straight to hell."

Her voice rose. Her hands twisted at the sauce-red paper towels, twisted and twisted until her hands were stained red. "Sometimes," Diana raged, "I wish I could make her *pay*. I could, you know—"

Cass tripped over and shook Diana's arm. "Snap out of it," she cried.

Diana blinked at Cass. She shook her head. "Oh, boy," she groaned. "Me and my terrible temper."

She looked down at the mess on the floor, then at us, and shook her head again. "Mom is *such* a perfectionist." She sighed. "She's a control freak, and she drives me crazy. Meg, thanks for offering to help, but I'd better do this myself."

I said that was fine, and she went, "C'mon, let's forget it, 'kay, and get with the pizzas. I'm sorry I was such a crab, Meg. Forgive me?"

She looked a little embarrassed. Her eyes were frank and clear. Impossible, I told myself.

It couldn't possibly be that when Rea's *abuelita* had spoken of a wicked angel, she had meant Diana *Angeli*.

SIX

BUT THAT WAS crazy. It was such a lame idea that I felt guilty even thinking about it.

I mean, here was Diana, eager to make up for her few seconds of bad temper. She helped me build my pizza, sat beside me as we ate our masterpieces, bubbly and hot from the oven. Later we moved to Diana's personal den, which was twice as big as our living room, and listened to more Aerosmith and Sheryl Crow. Diana, Vi, Karen, and I hung out while B.K. and Cass snuggled together into a couch in a corner of the room, and Kenny beat time to the music with whatever he could get his hands on.

A good afternoon—and when Kenny had driven Karen and me home, I was even more psyched to see Mom's car in the driveway. Inside the house Mimi was playing Lizst's Tarantella, and Mom was fixing dinner.

"How was the party?" Mimi called as I came in.

I said, fine, feeling really fine, *now,* and went to help Mom in the kitchen, where, wrapped in Mimi's music, we chopped and sautéed and grilled. As we worked together I found myself contrasting my mother with the glamorous Mrs. Angeli. Mom in her jeans and a scruffy sweatshirt, her hair a little mussed—when I tried picturing her poised in white and silver gauze as Diana the Huntress, the idea made me laugh out loud.

"Had fun this afternoon, huh?" Mom grinned.

She herself had had a good day at the store. A lot of new customers had come in, including a few who would definitely be regulars. Sales were picking up. "I feel really good about it," she said as we sat down to eat, "so I thought I'd come home and celebrate by being with you all. Now, tell me—how was your day?"

"It would seem you had fun," Mimi put in. "It was good to see Karen again, and that young fellow who came with her was quite personable." She paused, trying for his name, and said instead, "I'll bet he talks and jiggles around to conceal an inferiority complex."

"My mother the shrink," Mom joked, and gave her wonderful, catchy laugh.

I felt so happy. This was the way things had been before the pressures of running the store, before Mimi started getting confused. Wishing Dad were here to share this old-time happiness, I described the Angelis' big house, and the portrait of Diana's mother.

"Diana the Huntress," Mimi mused. "She was never one of my favorites. The goddess of the moon, the deity of the night, and mistress of all hidden things—she could be jealous, often cruel."

Her words brought up a sudden memory of Mrs. Angeli standing in her all-white kitchen. And on the heels of that image came another—the way Diana had twisted the crimson-stained paper towels until it seemed as if her hands were covered with blood.

Diana the huntress. Gorki had jumped up on my lap, so I stroked her automatically, and the warmth of my old cat felt good against the ripple of uneasiness that those images had brought.

"I almost forgot to ask about the funeral," Mom was saying. "That poor child. Something went really wrong for her."

And something *felt* wrong right now. I tried to ignore that prickling sense, but it wouldn't go away. Instead, I remembered the look in Diana's eyes when she'd said, "I'd like to make her pay."

The face of an angel, but inside she is a devil. Why should Rea's muttered words stick with me like heartburn? Maybe it was because Diana and her friends had warned me that Rea was a bad person. What I'd heard at the funeral today didn't tally with what the girls had said. Could they have been mistaken? Had they lied?

Why should they lie? For what reason? I took those questions to bed with me, and they followed me into vague, scary dreams. The worst one came near dawn with Rea standing in front of me asking sadly, "You, too, Meg? You, *too*?"

I was shaking when I woke up, and in the fragile dawnlight I swore to myself that I'd find out what was true about Rea and what wasn't. And for starters I decided to bike out to Creeden's Variety Store, where Rea had been caught shoplifting.

Creeden's opened at ten o'clock on Sunday. Around that time I rode my bike down to Six Corners, parked it, and went inside the variety store to find Jed Berringer stacking bottles of shampoo in a corner. "Do you work here?" I asked him, surprised.

"My cousin owns the store," Jed explained. "Once in a while he gets shorthanded or somebody calls in sick, so I help out. It's a family thing."

We chitchatted about running for a while and about our last biology lab, during which time I tried to put words to the question that was bothering me so much. "Do you know anything about—" I began, then stopped. That wasn't the way I wanted to put it. "I heard," I began, then stopped again, all tied up into knots.

Jed returned to stacking his shampoo bottles, patiently waiting for me to get my thoughts untwisted. When I finally managed to ask the question, he nodded. "Yeah, I remember. I was running that day and stopped here to get a Coke."

"I heard that Rea shoplifted and that the police came."

Jed looked at me curiously but said yes, that was the way it had gone down. "The cashier caught her with a bracelet worth a few bucks. My cousin's a madman on the subject of shoplifting, so he called the police."

I asked what had happened then, and Jed said Mrs. Alvarez had come down. "The cops actually didn't do anything to Rea, because my cousin didn't press charges—just warned her never to come back to the store. She was crying and saying she hadn't done anything, that she'd never seen the bracelet before in her life."

There was sympathy in his voice. "You believed her?" I asked.

"Yeah, I did. Rea wasn't like that." Jed paused. "Last year I was out of school for two weeks with the flu, and she went out of her way to help me catch up with our algebra class. She could explain stuff better than the teacher, even."

Yeah, she could—I felt a sudden tug of loss. "Was there anyone else here at the store that day?" I asked. Jed looked at me with a "what, are you kidding me?" look. "I meant, kids from your school."

Just then a lady came through the door of the store and started to look around. Jed went off to be helpful, and I strolled up the aisle till I came to the jewelry counter. As Jed had said, there weren't many expensive things there, but there was no clerk in attendance. Everything, except for the watches locked in the display case, was out in the open. It'd have been easy to reach out and palm something, slide it into a pocket.

"Why do you want to know all this stuff about Rea?" Jed asked, behind me. He'd come back and was continuing to stack. "And who told you about the shoplifting, anyway?"

I explained, and he sat back on his heels looking up at me, his forehead under his fair hair knotted into a frown. "Was Diana here that day?" I asked.

The frown deepened. "Yeah, now that you mention it. So were Cass and Vi—but then you know they're always together, right? You guys are friends."

His tone was carefully neutral, but living with Mimi had fine-tuned me to catching people's shifts of feeling. There was something about Diana and her girlfriends that Jed wasn't exactly comfortable with.

"They're friends of my friend Karen's, actually," I explained. Without commenting, he moved to another aisle and began stacking cups and plates. I followed him and started passing him stuff. "You knew Diana and the others at the middle school?" He said, still in that neutral tone, that he'd known them to say hi to. "Were they friendly with Rea?" I prodded again.

Jed stopped what he was doing and faced me, his dark

85

eyes almost stern. "Just what are you trying to say, Meg?"

His bluntness made me just as direct. "I didn't know Rea very well, but the things Diana and her friends told me about her don't sound right. I'm trying to get some answers."

He nodded, apparently accepting this. "I don't know about *friendly*. Diana and Cass took that algebra class with me and Rea," he told me. "Rea was the smartest kid in the class. Really, really smart. But shy. Hardly a word out of her. One time she got an A and the rest of us barely got by." Jed's lean face hardened into a frown. "Come to think of it, Diana didn't like that—no way. I mean, she tried to hide it, but she was pretty POed she'd got a C-plus. And Cass was pretty mad, too."

His words nudged another memory. The day the drugs were discovered in Rea's locker, Cass had come to lunch real late. The way she spoke and acted, it was like she'd accomplished a mission for Diana.

A mission planting dope in Rea's locker? Whoa, Meg, I warned myself, time out here. Put into words, my suspicion sounded paranoid, off base, a total stretch. There were ten different explanations for Cass coming late to lunch, none of which involved framing Rea for drug possession.

I needed to talk to someone who had known Rea well. Maybe a girlfriend from the seventh or eighth grade? But when I put this to Jed, he didn't know. Rea was shy at school and kept to herself, he said.

"The whole family's like that. Even in church, they didn't join anything. Not like Mom—she's on about forty committees." He paused as if chewing on a thought.

86

"If you really want to know about Rea, why not talk to Mrs. Alvarez?"

He said he had to get stuff from the back room, added that he'd catch me around school, and left me standing there. So, with the memory of Mrs. Alvarez's grief-ravaged face haunting me, I went outside and unlocked my bike. Jed was right. Rea's mother would have the answers to all my questions. But I was a stranger to her. Why should she even want to talk to me?

Okay, I had two choices: either I went home and forgot about it, or I barged in on Mrs. Alvarez's grief. I rode around Chisolm awhile, trying to decide what to do, and I still wasn't sure when I finally worked myself up to riding up the down-at-heel street where Rea's family lived. If no one was there, I told myself, I'd ride on by and forget the whole thing. And, see? The driveway was empty. Well, I'd tried. Now I could just turn around and go home—

A dusty blue Sentra, its front fender rusting, pulled up in the driveway, and Mrs. Alvarez got out. Dressed in a white blouse and black skirt, she looked smaller even than I remembered from the funeral, and her face looked so sad that I wanted to get *out* of there, fast. But by now it was too late. She'd seen me.

For a moment she just sort of blinked at me. Then she beckoned. "Come over here," she called.

Reluctantly, I rode up and she went, "You were there at the funeral, yes? Are you a friend of my Rea's?"

Her voice was low and husky as if from too many tears. The eyes into which I stared looked so empty. I introduced myself and mumbled, "We were lab partners in Ms. Llord's class."

To my surprise, Mrs. Alvarez's face actually brightened.

"Rea told me about you, Meg. She said you were a nice girl, that you ate lunch together." A pause during which her lips tried for a smile, couldn't make it. "Have you the time to come inside for a second?"

Taking my time because I needed to pull myself together, I parked my bike and locked it. Mrs. Alvarez watched me with a wordless patience that reminded me somehow of Rea. "It was kind of you to come," she said when I finally joined her on the porch.

"I'm really sorry about Rea," I said.

Tears softened the deadness in her eyes. "Come inside," she repeated. "The children have gone with a neighbor to a movie. My sister has returned to Puerto Rico, and my mother is sleeping."

The house was silent. It was a small house, but bright with September sunshine and, in spite of some friendly clutter, neat and clean. There were coloring books and crayons on the coffee table, a pair of well-used fluffy slippers near a rocking chair. A vase of carnations and lilies had been set up in a corner of the room in front of a shrine. There was a picture of Jesus exposing His bleeding heart, and another of Mary holding her baby, and a photo of Rea.

"That is my angel," Mrs. Alvarez said. She crossed herself, her fingers lingering on her lips as if blowing a kiss. "This is my sweet angel in heaven," she repeated.

Qué malo es el ángel. . . .

I sat down across from the little altar. "Would you like to have coffee?" Mrs. Alvarez asked mechanically, and I could hear the heaviness in her voice. It was as if making small talk was too hard for her right now. "Maybe a Coke?"

I said no, thanks. "I just wanted to tell you that I feel

88

really bad," I repeated awkwardly. "So do other kids at school."

"My Rea has not many friends. She is so shy." It was spooky the way Mrs. Alvarez kept referring to Rea as if she were still alive. "I do not think she knows many people at the new, big school."

I took a breath and plunged. "Lots of kids have asked about her," I babbled. "Jed Berringer, for one." Mrs. Alvarez nodded her recognition of that name. "And Diana Angeli—"

"*Ay, santísima,* are you that devil's friend?"

Into the emptiness of Mrs. Alvarez's eyes poured a blazing fury, and clenching her hands on her knees, she leaned forward to glare at me. I stammered, "No. Not her friend. I—I just thought Diana and Rea knew each other from middle school."

"Oh, she knows my Rea," Mrs. Alvarez said bitterly. "How well she knows! It is Diana and her two friends who drove my child to her death. Their teasing killed her."

Teasing? But kids ranked on other kids all the time. As I tried to explain to Mrs. Alvarez, some individuals thought they could make points for themselves by putting other kids down. If you walked up and down South Regional for a day, for instance, you'd hear a lot of mother-type insults, like, "Your mother's so fat she wears a parachute instead of a dress." And there were some unfortunate kids who were always getting picked on and ranked on by the likes of Darryl Haas.

"It's really lame, but it goes on all the time," I said. Mrs. Alvarez said that this wasn't the kind of teasing she meant. "But I never heard Diana say anything mean to Rea," I protested.

"She does not do or say anything to Rea in the open, not direct to the face. That is not her way. She spreads lies secretly about my daughter, gets her in trouble at school and outside school. One day in a store, the Angeli girl puts a bracelet in Rea's pocket and reports her to the cashier of the store. The police come, and Rea is treated like a shoplifter."

Something tense and waiting inside me seemed to click into place. So there *had* been something wrong. I hadn't imagined it. "You mean," I stammered, "it was D-Diana who—"

Mrs. Alvarez began to talk swiftly, mixing Spanish phrases in with the English as she became more excited. "Rea does not know Diana Angeli until she enters Chisolm Middle School and they have an algebra class together. *Ay, santísima,* it was a bad year for my Rea because that was the time my husband's trial is in the court."

She broke off, looked at me with eyes that reminded me of Rea's pleading eyes. "He is not a bad man, George, but he has a hot temper. At work, there is a fight, and the foreman hits George's friend and hurts him real bad. My George has a knife. He helps his friend, and he kills that foreman. It was accident, he never means to kill anyone, but he committed a crime, and he was given twenty years in prison. My Rea feels that hurt, here."

She put her hands on her own heart. Because of what happened to her father, Mrs. Alvarez said, Rea became even quieter and more introverted. But she kept up her grades, and scored miles above Diana and Cass in algebra.

"That is why they begin to torture her. Jealousy that she is more clever than the Angeli girl and her friend, the

90

small, pretty one. Vicious, the girls are! And when they see Rea is shy, she will not fight back, they torture her even more."

According to Mrs. Alvarez, Diana and Vi and Cass had made Rea's life totally miserable. "They tell lies about her, but so cleverly. Diana Angeli makes it sound that she doesn't *want* to say bad things about Rea."

I recalled Diana holding Vi back from talking about Rea's shoplifting. I remembered her sympathy. "She says terrible things so softly, even reluctantly, and so people believe her," Mrs. Alvarez said bitterly. "In this way rumors are made to sound like truths. Notes and letters are sent in Rea's name. Bad letters! *Santísima!* Soon no one wants to be friends with the 'bad' Rea Alvarez."

As I listened my stomach commenced to bunch into a tight knot. Mrs. Alvarez said that one time the girls had slipped a crib sheet into Rea's notebook and then "anonymously" told the teacher that Rea was cheating. Another time, Diana and her pals had spread the rumor that Rea was a boy-crazy slut, ready to make out with anything in pants.

"But how do you know they were doing all those things?" I interrupted.

"Rea caught the tall one, Vi, one time." Mrs. Alvarez's eyes burned with anger. "Rea saw Vi put a note in a boy's book. Rea pulled it out and saw a letter—a letter with many dirty words in it—signed with Rea's name. She brought it for me to see, and I went to talk to the principal, Mrs. Jameson."

But the principal hadn't done anything. There was no proof, she said, that Vi had written the note Rea had found. Mrs. Jameson needed solid evidence before confronting Diana and her friends.

91

"What Mrs. Jameson meant was that everybody at school knows Diana," Mrs. Alvarez said. "Everyone likes her. Diana is the treasurer in the student council, president of one club, a big shot in another. Vi is glamorous and everybody admires her style. Cass is voted Miss Congeniality in the middle-school yearbook. And it was these popular girls' word against Rea's."

"But didn't the principal listen to *you*?" I cried, and Mrs. Alvarez pushed air impatiently through her nose.

"Mr. Julius Angeli, big CEO of Lartheon Electronics, went to see the principal and told her that he wouldn't tolerate any bad words against his daughter. He is important and rich, so naturally Mrs. Jameson listened to him."

No one had listened to Mrs. Alvarez, who was neither important nor rich. No one had believed Rea, not even me. My heart had begun to pound so heavily that I felt a little sick. "I have to go," I said.

Mrs. Alvarez hadn't even heard me. "Ay, now I see that it was my fault," she went on, and now the anger in her voice had changed to pain. "We should have moved away when the teasing became so bad. But I was afraid to lose my work at Nallie's Restaurant. It is hard to get good jobs now. And we have a second mortgage on this house." She paused a little before adding the final argument. "And Chisolm is close to—to where my husband is."

She got up, walked painfully across to the little altar, and picked up Rea's photograph. "She says, 'Mama, don't you think of moving, I can bear it because none of it is true.' She hoped that after she started at the regional school, things would get better. And it *was* better. She was so happy when she told me she had met you and that you were going to be friends."

92

When I thought of how I'd let Rea down that last day of her life, I wanted to cry, but that wouldn't have done a diddly bit of good or made me feel any less guilty.

Rea'd wanted to be a teacher, and instead she was dead at fifteen because she couldn't stand to be tormented any longer. I didn't even question that Mrs. Alvarez was telling the truth. Everything she'd told me fit too well with the few things that I already suspected.

"They can't get away with it," I said aloud. "I won't let them."

Mrs. Alvarez put Rea's photo down. "They are clever, those girls, and they are vicious. Be careful, Meg. If they sense you are against them, they will hurt you, too."

Coming home from Mrs. Alvarez's, I found Mom sitting at the kitchen table. A full cup of coffee sat in front of her, and she was stirring and stirring it. When she saw me come through the door, she raised her head and gave me a half smile.

"Hi," she said.

"Why aren't you at the store?" I asked, and her smile faded.

"The director of Meadowriver just phoned me. They have an unexpected opening."

For a minute what she was saying didn't connect. "Mimi?" I finally whispered. Mom nodded. "But—but you *can't,* Mom. She's been all right this past week. And last night, when we had dinner together, she was really with it, wasn't she? She was the way she used to be."

"We put her name on the list, Meg, okay? Two patients died, one was discharged." Mom didn't meet my eyes. "I guess you're never ready. I thought I was, but I'm not."

93

How about *Mimi* being ready? I wanted to shout, but then I saw the tears shining in Mom's eyes and knew that she was under a lot of pressure, too. "What did Dad say?" I whispered.

"They called us at the store, and I came right home. Dad said he'd close an hour or so early so we can tell Mama together." She looked down at her coffee cup. "Once the decision is made, it's best to follow through right away."

Feeling light-headed and sick, as if I'd run for hours in the heat, I went upstairs. Mimi's door was open, and she was lying on her bed, her hands folded on her stomach. "Hi," I said.

"Hey, there." If she had been vague today, it'd have been easier to take, but she was sharply in focus. "How was your ride?"

"Oh, okay," I said. "I'll tell you about it later."

Then I ran to my own room and shut the door because I didn't want her to hear me bawling as I was sure to do if I stuck around. Meadowriver, I thought. To Mimi, Meadowriver was sure to sound as bad as Devil's Island.

I hadn't gone with the folks when they took Mimi on a tour of Meadowriver so that she could get used to the idea. Mimi hadn't said a word about that outing, and I really hadn't wanted to know, but now I tried to remember everything Mom had said about Meadowriver. It was a wonderful facility, she'd enthused, specializing in dementia and Alzheimer's patients. They'd give Mimi the help and attention she needed.

"It stinks," I muttered.

Usually, Sunday afternoon is a favorite time for me. Homework's been done, and Monday is still a ways off. But today I sat staring out of the window, not having the energy to go for a run, not even having the strength to turn on my music.

I was still sitting when I heard a car drive into the driveway and then my folks' voices in the kitchen downstairs. They talked for a while and then Mom called us down for supper.

As usual, I stopped first at Mimi's room. "Hey, time for dinner," I told her in what I hoped was a cheerful voice.

"About time," Mimi said. She got up from bed and shook her head a little. "Clearing cobwebs," she explained apologetically. "I've been lying down too long."

Mom had made Mimi's favorite—beef stew with dumplings—the condemned woman's last meal. With my appetite stopped cold by the knot in my throat, I watched my grandmother walk to her chair and seat herself with straight-backed grace. I thought of how she must have looked when she was young, striding up the Alps with her long, jet-black hair blowing like a banner in the wind.

Mimi was hungry tonight, which was a good thing because nobody else ate much. I even turned away apple pie, which I normally adored, and my stomach knotted when Dad cleared his throat.

"Mother," he began, then stopped. "Mother, we need to talk."

"I seem to be in trouble," Mimi came back, sharp and clear. "Am I?"

"No, Mama, not at all," Mom said. She swallowed and started talking really fast. "The director of Meadowriver called me today. You remember the place, don't you? We went there together."

"The nursing home," Mimi said. Her face suddenly

95

went tense, and she sat up even straighter in her chair. In a toneless voice she then added, "I see."

"Mama, we've talked about it, haven't we? We went to see the place together." Mom was near tears. "They have doctors and nurses there who can help you, okay? And—and there's a baby grand there. And do you remember the beautiful atrium, full of flowers? You liked that nice day nurse supervisor on the first floor."

Tenser, straighter, Mimi folded her lips into silence. Mom went on desperately, "You know you get confused, sometimes. We're not here all day and can't help you. And—and you'll be home for dinner Sundays, and we'll visit you each day. Mama, no one *wants* this—"

"It's not as if you were going to the ends of the earth," Dad added, too heartily. "This is for your own safety, Mother."

I couldn't stand it. I excused myself, carried my plate and glass to the kitchen, then went upstairs. Once in my room, I cranked up my CD player and put on earphones so I could drown out what they were saying downstairs.

Life absolutely wasn't fair. Unfair that Mimi, who was so independent and smart and full of music, was being sent to a nursing home. That my folks were so uptight with making a living at that darn store that they didn't have time to be a family anymore. And now our "family" would no longer include Mimi—

I couldn't stand it. So, to dull the edges of my misery over Mimi, I forced myself to focus on someone else: Rea. And from Rea my mind skipped to Karen, who liked Diana, admired Vi. Munch seemed so close to those girls, but maybe that was how Diana set up her victims. Suddenly I wondered if Karen could be in some kind of danger from her so-called friends.

Maybe I should warn Munch? But the thought drifted off as I heard Mimi come up the stairs. She walked slowly, shuffling like a very old woman. I heard her hesitate by my door and held my breath. If she came in to talk about Meadowriver, could I bear it?

But she walked by, and I felt a cowardly relief, for which I hated myself. Instead of being glad that I didn't have to face her now, I knew that I should go to her and hold her hand, swear that I'd come see her every single day—

I was saved by the telephone ringing. " 'S happening?" Karen bubbled.

"Everything—too much," I said. "Can you come over?"

Munch asked, was I kidding? "This is *Sunday,*" she reminded me. "Moms wouldn't let me go out on a Sunday if I had an invitation from the president. You come on down here—and tell her we're doing homework, 'kay?"

As I hung up the phone I heard Mimi moving around her room, and I could hear her talking to herself. I peeked through her door and saw that she'd started to empty stuff from her closet and drawers onto her bed. She was shaking her head and talking to herself, and the slow, sleepwalking way in which she moved made me want to bawl.

So I pulled on my sweats and my reflectors and running shoes and went downstairs, where I told Mom that I was going to Karen's. I didn't give her time to yes or no, just raced out of there and down the road. But I couldn't outrun the memory of Mimi's face or the sound of her voice.

"It sucks," I snarled.

The crescent moon—the same sliver of light that had

circled Mrs. Angeli's forehead in her portrait—swung above me. Around me as I ran, the night felt September cool. It was a beautiful night and I hated it. Hated the world and the laws of nature that said people had to grow old and be shut away from their families.

Karen looked surprised when she opened the door for me at her house. "You must have really *booked*," she exclaimed. "You got here in less than five minutes." Then she took a look at my face. "Are you okay?"

"No," I almost shouted.

Munch shushed me hastily. "C'mon up to my room," she whispered. "We're supposed to be doing homework, 'member?"

Karen's mother was in the den, reading. She was an older version of Karen, small and chubby with dark brown curls and eyes out of which all joy and pleasure had been scrubbed away. "Homework," Mrs. Tierney repeated, those mean eyes boring into us. "That's all, girls. This is the Lord's Day."

Karen's own face was gloomy as we climbed the stairs. "Nag, nag, nag," she mumbled. "I can't wait till I am in college and *out* of here. I wish Moms would send me to live with Daddy, but she'd rather die first because that might make him too happy."

She drew a deep breath, plopped down at her dresser, and picked up a toothbrush with which she commenced to brush her eyebrows. "Vi says you have to direct the brows *down* till you can see the natural brow line," she explained. "So, okay, tell me what's got you so rattled? Is it your grandma again?"

I said yes, that was part of it, and told her about Meadowriver. Munch listened, said how tough it was, and then added hopefully, "But maybe your grandmother'll like it there. And Meadowriver is in Chisolm, so me and you can go visit her after school and then stop in at Diana's on the way home. 'Kay?"

She'd given me the opening I needed. "Munch," I said, "how well do you know Diana and the other two girls?"

Munch put down her toothbrush and turned to look at me in surprise. "Say, what?"

"I mean," I began again, "you and I have known each other practically all our lives, right?" She nodded. "We know everything about each other. What do you *really* know about those girls?"

Round face expressing total bafflement, Karen just stared at me. I next told her about what the old lady had said about the bad angel at the funeral, and Munch said, even more bewildered, "She meant the devil. Us Catholics believe in the devil. Mom figures he's forever behind me, switching his little tail and tempting me. What's the devil got to do with Diana?"

So I told her what I'd been doing today. I told her about Jed at the store, and then about my stopping to see Mrs. Alvarez. "You went to see *who*?" Karen demanded.

"I went to see Rea's mother. I wanted to know about Rea and she told me. She said that Diana and Cass and Vi had tormented Rea all through middle school—"

Which was as far as I got before Karen jumped to her feet and stared at me as if I'd grown a second head. "She's crazy," Karen cried. "You're nuts, too, believing all that sick stuff."

"Mrs. Alvarez didn't sound crazy," I interrupted. "She sounded like she knew exactly what she was talking about." As I cataloged the abuse that Diana and the other girls had dumped on Rea, Karen's face hardened into a mask of total denial.

"I don't believe you," she exclaimed. "I don't want to hear this."

She covered her ears with her hands. "Listen to me," I cried, but she turned her back on me. I tried turning her around, but Karen shook me off. "I don't say I *believe* it," I said, raising my voice so she was sure to hear me. "But don't you think there are a lot of coincidences? Like the girls being in the store when Rea got arrested for shoplifting. She'd *never* been in trouble before."

"It's all lies." Karen squeezed her eyes tight shut. See no evil, hear no evil. "Vi was right."

"Right? What do you mean, right?" I demanded. "What are you talking about?"

"You're jealous," she accused. "You're jealous because you think I'm better friends with them than with you. That's why you're trying to make trouble." Karen snapped open her eyes, glared at me. "Just cut it out," she warned.

I took a deep breath, tried again. "Munch, listen to me," I said. "I'm not trying to make trouble for anyone. I'm trying to find out what happened to Rea."

"You *know* what happened to her. It was her own fault. She was doing all kinds of crazy stuff! Drugs in her locker—"

"She was no druggie. Someone planted that stuff in her locker."

"—and those disgusting flyers," Munch went on as if I hadn't spoken. "That girl was Looney Tunes. She was *sick*."

I argued that that nude photograph of Rea could've been computer-generated. "I saw it on a TV cop show, one time," I told Karen. "You take somebody's head and stick it on somebody else's body—"

"Shut up, shut *up*," Karen screamed at me.

There was a silence. Into it we heard Mrs. Tierney call querulously, "Girls? What is going *on* up there?"

Glaring, panting, Karen lowered her voice. "I don't believe a word you said," she hissed. "Rea Alvarez was a slut and a thief and a junkie, and you're trying to make it like Diana's to blame. Well, if you can think crazy things like that, you're not my friend."

She whipped out a hand, grabbed me by my shoulders, and shoved me toward the door. "Just get out of here, Meg Fairling."

SEVEN

IN STUNNED SILENCE I plodded home, dragged myself up to my room, slapped on my earphones, and cranked Pearl Jam so loud that my ears were blasted. It didn't help.

Mimi'd once told me that the thing that bugs you the most usually has a grain of truth embedded in it. Okay, face it, Meg, Vi was right. I *was* jealous that Karen had fallen all over herself when Diana and her pals had looked her way. But that wasn't why I'd warned her. Well, maybe it was *part* of the reason, but not the whole reason. If Mrs. Alvarez was right about those girls, Munch was playing with fire. I worried about her because I cared what happened to her and—and I totally *hated* what had happened between us tonight.

I pulled off my earphones and let silence stun me. "We'll make up tomorrow," I assured Gorki, who'd hopped onto my lap. "It'll be okay tomorrow."

But when I awoke, it was to the darkest, meanest-looking Monday I'd ever seen. A storm was moving up the Atlantic coast, and New England was getting fringe benefits of thunder and cold rain. I dressed to the growls of distant thunder, and when I got out into the hall, Mimi's door was open.

There she sat with her belongings piled up on her narrow bed and on the floor, sat and stared at her hands, which were clenched in her lap. "I don't want to go anywhere," she declared. "They say they're taking me to a home where I can be cared for. But this *is* my home."

Her voice was flat-out accusing. The anger in it made the lump in my throat solidify to ice. Come on, Mimi, you'll like it at Meadowriver, they have activities and fun—words rose to my lips to be beaten down by Mimi's stern gaze. Stupid words that meant nothing. Why would she love it?

She stamped her foot and glared at me. "*This* is where I live."

I went over to her and gave her a big hug. It was the only thing I could think of to do, but she didn't hug me back. "Mimi, don't," I whispered against her ear. "Please, don't. I hate it, too, but—but we'll see each other every day. It won't be so bad, really. Honest, it won't. Sa' right, Mimi?"

No response. She just sat there, angry and confused. Miserable to the bones, I tore myself away and ran down the stairs to the kitchen, where Dad sat shrouded in his newspaper. Mom stood by the stove, not doing anything, just staring into the backyard, where the blue jays were feeding in the rain. Their angry screeches brought Gorki, tail twitching, to the window.

Gorki was an old cat, and she'd enjoy her uncomplicated life until it became too painful. Then she'd be mercifully put down. Gorki could be lucky—hating that dismal thought, hating what was happening, I grabbed a glass of juice and made it out of the door without a word to anyone.

Outside, it was raining hard. When I got to the bus stop, Karen was already there, cocooned in her slicker. She ignored me.

"Look," I said, "I'm sorry if I made you mad last night. I just told you because I wanted you to know what was going on."

Pointedly, she turned her head away. "Munch," I pleaded, "let's not fight, okay? Mimi's going to Meadowriver today. For Pete's sakes," I cried, "talk to me."

"It's too late," she said, and turned her back, leaving me feeling as cold and raw as the weather.

With that rawness inside me, I went to school and sat through homeroom staring at the crazy doodles somebody had etched onto the desk. I didn't feel any better during English, and when I walked through the door into biology class, I had a spooky feeling that Rea was somewhere around.

Chill, Meg, get a hold of yourself—warning myself not to come unglued, I went over to the table near the windows, where our lab books were stacked. Mine wasn't there, even though I distinctly remembered putting it—

"Oh, jeez," I exclaimed.

My lab notebook was lying on the edge of the table, and it was sopping wet. I snatched it up, saw that my notes were smudged and unreadable. "Double rats," I moaned.

Just then a drop of water fell on my arm. I glanced up and saw that one of Ms. Llord's hanging plants was dripping down on me.

"Whoa," Jed went. He'd slung his books onto his desk and had come over to stare at the mess in my hands. "What happened?"

104

Instead of answering him, I jumped up on a chair and felt the earth in the pot. It was sopping. I checked out the other plants around the room, but they hadn't been watered. "Someone overwatered this plant," I sputtered to Jed, who was watching me as if I'd totally lost it. "Somebody wanted to ruin my lab notes."

As I spoke Darryl Haas walked into the room. "Did'ja take your notebook into the bathtub, Meg?" he snickered.

"Did *you* do this?" But I knew better. Darryl might've thrown my notebook into the garbage, but he didn't have the brains to think of overwatering a plant so that the overflow would "accidentally" damage my notes.

My thoughts were interrupted by Ms. Llord marching into the classroom. She came over to us and clicked her tongue at the state of my lab notebook. "Carelessness," she rapped out. Then, frowning, she asked who had moved the hanging plant because the light there was wrong for ivy geraniums.

And of course my lab notes would have to be recopied. I thought of the hours of work I'd put into that notebook and felt close to crying. But Ms. Llord didn't leave any time for such foolishness. Pitilessly, she plunged us into cell membranes.

After biology I went to my locker to get my books for social studies and found that I was missing my *Early America* textbook. I was sure that I'd left it in my locker on Friday, but the way things were going today, I couldn't be sure. So I went to class without the book and got into trouble because Mr. Jacobs was giving us an open-book quiz.

I was still trying to remember where I could have left my book when lunchtime came around. As I went down to the cafeteria Vi was making her way to a table where

Cass and B.K. were already sitting. She looked back over her shoulder, glanced at me, and then turned away as if she didn't even know me.

I heard a familiar giggle and saw Karen bounce in between Diana and Kenny. Not one of them even glanced my way, a clear sign that Karen had broadcasted everything I'd said last night to her new best friends.

It was what I'd expected, but even so, I felt crushed. And as I sat down by myself at a table, it hit me that I was acting just as Rea had done the day I'd chosen to sit with Karen's new friends. "Whatever goes around comes around," I told myself aloud, quoting Mimi.

Mimi . . .

The deep breath I took was heavy with the sting of tears. Then I saw Karen looking my way, and the tears dried up, quick. I picked up a piece of rubbery pizza, thinking, no way was I going to let Munch think she was making me miserable enough to cry.

Just then Jed walked by with a group of guys from the boys' cross-country team and stopped at my table to tell me he was sorry about my lab book. "You can copy my notes if you want," he offered.

I thanked him gratefully. "You don't have a partner yet, right?" he then asked. "Maybe Ms. Llord'll leave us paired up. Anybody'd be better than Darryl."

I said thanks a heap, whereupon he did one of his lightning subject changes. "Did you see Mrs. Alvarez yesterday?"

While I nodded, I could feel the press of hostile eyes behind me. "She answered most of my questions," I said. "I just don't know what to do with the answers."

Jed said he'd catch me later and walked off to join his

106

pals. Feeling more isolated than before, I gave up on my pizza and got up to go.

Without looking their way, I knew that everybody at Diana's table was watching me walk across the cafeteria. So, let them watch! Moving deliberately so's to show them I didn't care, I started to tip my mostly uneaten food into the trash—then stopped dead. An *Early America* textbook was lying buried in the garbage.

I reached into the trash, pulled out the book. Streaks of mustard, red blobs of ketchup decorated it, and congealed grease was hardening over the pages. I didn't have to turn to the name on the book cover to know it was mine.

There was a suppressed snicker behind me. I turned around quick, but nobody at Diana's table was looking my way. I felt sick as I wiped the pages as clean as I could on a handful of napkins. No need to guess who'd done this or to ask who'd ruined my lab notebook. Karen's new friends were getting even with me for asking questions about them.

The second snicker was the last straw. I whirled on my heel and, carrying my disasterized book, marched up to the table. "You think you're being funny?" I snarled at them all.

For a second nobody said anything. Then: "Are you talking to us?" Vi drawled.

I was so mad that I was shaking. "I don't know which of you did this," I raged, "but it was a dumb move. You may think you can do stuff to me like you did to Rea, but you're wrong. I'm not about to let you creeps get away with diddly."

Kenny made a snorting sound. I whipped around to

him and vowed, "If I hear anything more out of you, you'll have my fist up your allergies."

"Hey, what *is* this?" macho-man B.K. huffed. "What're you in our face for, you geek? Get out of here."

"Yeah, just butt out," Kenny sneered. "You weren't invited."

He started to get up, but Diana put out a hand and held him back. "She's acting crazy," she said.

With narrowed eyes, I stared down at Diana Angeli. Her clear green eyes held annoyance, bewilderment—*hurt*. The face of an angel, but the heart of a devil— Rea, you were so right.

"Don't give me that innocent look," I snapped at her. "You know exactly what I'm talking about."

"No, I don't," she replied coolly, "but since you're here, I want to say that I don't appreciate the lies you told Karen about us. I think you're sick, Meg, but I feel sorry for you, too."

I was sick? *Me?* Hot rage bubbled into me. Out of the corner of my eye I saw that a lunch monitor was walking our way. I lowered my voice.

"Mess with me," I swore, "and you're the one who's going to need pity."

Diana turned to Karen. "I think your friend has a problem," she said, and Munch shook her head so hard that her curls jounced.

"She's not *my* friend," she said.

The next two days passed like beats of the funeral march that Mimi used to play sometimes—slow and heavy. At school, I had a wary eye turned on Diana's group, but so far they'd kept out of my way. I figured that after my outburst at the cafeteria, they were reacting the way bullies usually do—show some fight, and they back off and leave you alone.

So much for school. After classes, there was Prud-homme's chain gang, which I now almost enjoyed for the simple reason that it put off the time when I'd have to come home and face Mimi's empty room. Mom kept the door to that room shut, but I could feel the emptiness that lay behind the closed door.

I'd gone to see Mimi at Meadowriver the first day she was admitted but hadn't been able to visit with her because she was being "evaluated." Next day Mom took me with her when she went around seven-thirty in the evening, but by then Mimi had had her dinner and was in bed. She was sleepy and vague, not like herself at all, and Mom said that they had her on medication.

Meaning that my grandmother was heavily sedated. Mom couldn't fool me—I'd seen *One Flew over the Cuckoo's Nest* one time late on the Movie Channel. That night, after the folks went to bed, I crept into Mimi's room, curled up on her cold, empty bed, and cried my eyes out.

Next morning I went to school with a headache, which got worse as the day progressed. By third period, social studies, I was aching to sleep it off. So I took my usual seat in the back, propped open my book, and was just starting to let my eyes glaze over when our teacher made this sputtering noise.

Astonished, I came awake to see that Mr. Jacobs had become as red as a beet. Making gobbling sounds in his nose and throat, he glared at me. "How *dare* you, young woman?" he wheezed. "How *dare* you!"

Had he seen me prepared to snork off? But most kids slept in his class, and he hadn't seemed to mind. In fact he'd seemed downright relieved sometimes. So when he rasped, "Meg, stay after class. I want to talk to you," I was totally baffled.

Next to me, Doris Leo rolled her eyes. "Luckeee," she snuffled. "I'd give *anything* to have him keep *me* after class."

But there was nothing in Mr. Jacobs's treatment of me that made me feel privileged. He ignored me all through class, and when the bell finally rang and I went to stand by his desk, he continued to ignore me. Finally, when all the kids had gone, he dragged a piece of paper out of his desk drawer and practically threw it at me.

"Did you write this?" he demanded.

Bewildered, I began to read what appeared to be a note, but a few sentences into it, my ears started to sizzle. I wanted to quit reading, but my eyes kept whizzing from one obscene word to the next.

"Don't deny that you wrote this filth." Mr. Jacobs's high voice sounded like the buzz of a wasp. "It was lying on top of the attendance sheet. It's your writing."

It *looked* like my writing, I had to admit that, but I could never in a million years have written something like this. I didn't even know what some of the words meant. I tried to tell Mr. Jacobs this, but he was sputtering on and on and totally ignored me.

"It's the most—it's the worst—how could you even think of such filth?" he ranted. "I should take you to the principal, but I can't bear to have him read— I mean, it's hard enough to be a teacher without having to—never, *never* let me see anything like this again!"

110

Then he tore the note into a hundred pieces and tossed them into the wastepaper basket. "I didn't write that," I protested.

Mr. Jacobs didn't believe me. I could see that from the loathing look he gave me. I didn't blame him; if someone had written me a note like that, I'd have thought him slime, too. "But I didn't write it." Fear and disgust made my voice shake as I repeated, "Honestly, I didn't."

He who excuses himself accuses himself. . . . "Just get out of my sight," Mr. Jacobs snarled.

Some older kids were coming into the class for the next period. Among them was B.K. As I hurried past him he oinked, pig style. Normally I'd have ignored his juvenile attempt at humor, but just now I wanted to take his head off.

Muttering to myself, I plodded through the busy corridor to my locker. When I'd squared off with Diana and the others in the lunchroom, I hadn't really thought of what I was up against. I'd thought—I don't know what I'd thought. Now I realized what Rea had been through. Now I remembered her mother's warning.

It was pretty obvious that Diana'd chosen me for her next victim. Well, she could save it—she wasn't going to break me. Not today, not ever. No way were these freaks going to win.

A familiar twittering voice broke into my thoughts, and I saw Cass walking ahead of me. She was talking to another girl, her small, curly head cocked to one side, but as if she'd sensed me staring, she turned and looked at me. Looked, smiled at me, and then tripped off into her classroom.

111

I stood where I was with my heart beating a mile a minute. With anger and—let's face it, Meg, be honest—from fear. Cass's wicked little smile had made the goose-flesh dance up and down my spine.

I kept seeing that malicious smirk all day, which crawled by with the speed of a snail. Then, after a practice that was vicious even by his standards, our coach allowed that even though we were freshmen scum, there was *some* hope for a few of us to make it to the league meet in October.

He looked straight at me as he spoke, but my spurt of hope was quickly doused by weariness. Wobble-kneed, I rode my bike home into the heavy silence of our house. No melodic Chopin, no moody Rachmaninoff greeted me, and there was only Gorki twitching her tail beside Mimi's cracked-open room. She meowed and yawned, and the sound was so normal that for a second I was caught in a Trekkie time warp. For a second I almost hoped that everything that had happened was a dream and that if I opened her door, Mimi would be there.

Emptiness greeted me as I pushed open the door. Mimi had taken her quilt and her photographs with her, so it looked like a stranger's room. On her night table only her empty Steuben vase remained to wink rainbows across her books.

Slowly, I walked over to the books and pulled one out. It was a book of poems, and it fell open to show a four-leaf-clover bookmark I'd made for her in second grade. This yellowed good-luck charm marked a poem that began: "Do not go gentle into that good night—"

She'd said something like that the day at the music store, so she'd had to have known that she was walking steadily toward that "good night." "Mimi," I whispered as rainbows formed a nimbus through my tears. "Don't you give up and start getting gentle now."

Just then the phone began to shrill. I picked it up and some guy said, "Meg?" I said, yes it was, and he purred, "So, when can we get it on, babe?"

Thoughts of Mimi had dulled my brain. I asked, what was he talking about, and the guy went, "You tell me, babe. You name the place and time."

I hung up. The phone rang again almost instantly. "Listen, Meg, you shouldn't hang up," the same guy said. He sounded a little irritated. "I'm interested in partying with you, all right?"

If this was a joke, it wasn't funny. Once again, I slammed the phone down on his ear. The phone rang twice more, but I just picked up the receiver and hung up, then left the receiver off until my folks got home.

For once, they were early—and mad at me. "What were you thinking of, tying up the phone line?" Dad demanded as soon as he walked through the door. "We kept calling you and getting a busy signal. Your mother was sure something was wrong at home."

"There is," I began.

Nobody heard me because Mom had already jumped in with, "It isn't like you to be so thoughtless, Meg. That's why we got call waiting, so none of us would tie up the phone. What were you doing, talking to two friends at the same time?"

Then Dad added that they'd had to close the store early to get back home and check on me. Well, thanks a lot, folks. My world is coming apart and you're worried about closing your dumb store an hour early.

"You never listen to me," I cried, and then Mom said something, and I snapped back, and Dad snarled that if I didn't have any respect, I could go to my room.

Just then, the phone rang. I jumped for it, but Dad snatched up the receiver. I held my breath until he began discussing something about the store.

"It's been brutal all day," Mom said, half apologizing. "We've ordered some products from a new line, and there've been nothing but problems with it. Now the company that sold the brand is giving us a hard time on returns."

Which explained their bad moods. Understanding but still resentful, I looked at Dad, who was still on the phone, and saw that he was looking more tired than usual. "I had a bad day, too—" I began.

But Mom wasn't listening to me. "I stopped and saw your grandmother," she interrupted. "She seemed better tonight. I think she's adjusting."

Which meant that Mimi had been quiet and meek and doped up again. I didn't ask questions because I didn't want to know. And later that night, when the phone rang again, and a whispery voice crooned, "We're going to get it on, Meggy!" I took the phone off the hook again.

Finally, there was peace—but the quiet didn't help me sleep. Rain had commenced to fall, and the raindrops drummed down noisily on the eaves as all night I twisted and turned, trying to find a comfortable spot on the pillow. Tried to find some peaceful spot inside my head where I could shut out all that was happening.

Naturally, Diana and her pals were behind my getting those obscene calls, and by now they might have put together a flyer like the one they'd circulated about Rea. That thought made me feel so sick that I decided to tell my folks what was going on. I mean, this whole thing was too big for me to take on alone.

But by morning I'd changed my mind again because I'd remembered what poor Mrs. Alvarez had told me. Mom and Dad couldn't help me if I had no proof to back me up. It'd be my word against Diana's. Even if my parents went to MacMasters, how could they convince him I was telling the truth?

So I said nothing. I went to school braced for trouble and found it in a gauntlet of sniggers and whistles as I walked to homeroom. Then, when I was getting books from my locker, somebody grabbed my boobs from behind.

I hauled off and whaled him with the books I held. He yelped and staggered backward, massaging his arm, and I glared at this short, squat kid with zits all over his face.

"If you ever try that again," I snarled, "you'll be looking for your teeth on the floor."

"You're just getting what you want," he growled under his breath, but he took off pretty quick. Another guy, a beefy upperclassman, whistled loudly as I walked to class.

"Hey, party girl"—he snickered—"want to party with me?"

That was the way it went through the first two periods. Then, when I walked into biology class, Darryl Haas slouched by me, leering. "How about we get it *on*, Meg-gy?" he invited.

"Take a hike, Haas." Jed had walked up to us. Darryl jutted his jaw as if he was going to make something of it, spotted Ms. Llord in the doorway of the room, and reluctantly lumbered toward his desk. "Was that jerk bothering you?" Jed demanded.

"Him and a whole bunch of others," I muttered.

Silently Jed pulled an index card from his book and handed it to me. On the card was my name, and under it my phone number and the neatly printed words: FOR A GOOD TIME IN THE SACK OR ANYWHERE ELSE, CALL ME.

Feeling the bile seep up into my throat, I tore the card into a million pieces. My face felt barbecue hot. "I didn't write this," I choked.

"I *know* that." I looked up at Jed, saw that his dark eyes were angry. "Nobody in her right mind would do a thing like this."

"They're doing what they did to Rea—" but just then the period bell went and Ms. Llord called us to order.

All through class, I ground my teeth wondering how many of the guys in the school had gotten my so-called ad. No wonder the phone had rung off the hook last night!

Diana had done herself proud. But no way could I believe that Karen was in on this mean trick. Munch just didn't know what her new friends were really like, I thought, miserably. Munch was so impressed with Diana that she couldn't believe Diana had any faults.

The rain cut our practice short. This left me with a huge gob of time on my hands and a problem. Did I go

116

see Mimi, who might be sedated and out of it, or go home and wait for the phone to ring?

Chisolm was a big town. I'd left my bike at home, so I ran the six miles to Meadowriver, which was a big, brick building sitting on several acres of prettily landscaped grounds. Butterflies danced around purple asters and coppery marigolds, and on the neatly whitewashed front porch, old folks were gossiping.

Mimi wasn't among them, and my heart sank. But on my way to her room, I ran into Ruth Winton, the day nurse supervisor. "She's not in her room," she informed me. "Keep walking past the atrium and you'll find her." Then she winked.

It soon became obvious why Ruth had looked so pleased. As I progressed down the first-floor hall I heard the piano spinning off on "Alexander's Rag-time Band." Picking up speed, I followed the music to a largish room that was full of hanging plants and comfortable chairs. There were a dozen people in the room, all of them clustered around the baby grand, where Mimi was really making those notes vibrate.

Talk about a friendly audience—this crew truly loved her. They hummed, they clapped, they tapped their feet. One old guy in a walker was actually trying to dance, and a fat lady with a jet-black beehive hairdo was snapping her fingers and wriggling all over.

The hard, cold lump I'd carried inside me for the last few days dissolved in a rush of happiness as Mimi ended up with a bunch of chords that made the windows vibrate. Her audience clapped and stomped and cheered, and Ms. Beehive Hairdo boomed, "That sure is wonderful, lamb. I do wish I could play the piano."

"It's not so difficult. I'll teach you, Vera," Mimi said. She turned to say something else, spotted me, and broke into a wide grin. "Meg!" she called. "Come over here and meet these nice people."

Prideful, proprietary, she kept a hand on my arm as she introduced me. The beehive lady was Ms. Vera Pors, who'd been an insurance sales rep, and a damned good one at that, lamb. A delicate lady with blue-tinged white hair was Miss Harriway, Mr. Saito was the small gent in the blue V-necked sweater and tweed pants, and the old guy with the walker was Mr. Sulieman.

"Call me Silky, all my friends do," he told me. His smile split the most seamed and wrinkled face I'd ever seen, but his handshake was so strong that I almost yelped. "You're the runner. Cross-country, am I right?"

I nodded, and he beamed, pleased. "I can always tell. Got to be one to spot one, am I right? Once a distance runner, always a runner. Marathons were my thing—except now I feel more like dancing because your grandma plays like an angel. Am I right, Vera?"

The beehive lady roared with laughter, smashed Silky's skinny shoulder with a huge paw, and quoth that if he didn't watch out, lamb, she'd take him up on it. Then she shouted, "Now come on, all of you, and let Mimi talk with her little granddaughter."

Mimi smiled at me as her audience took themselves off, and we looked at each other until I felt my eyes grow misty. "Hey," I whispered.

"Hey, yourself." Mimi patted the piano seat next to her and slid her hands over some chords. "Now, *this* is more like a piano. Paganini Twenty-four, all right?"

She began one of the first duets we'd played together. It was an easy piece, but today my mind wasn't

118

on it, and my fingers kept slipping. "Don't let your fingers do all the work," Mimi advised. "Let the music flow from your shoulders down your arms. Lift your arms at the elbows and let your fingers hang loose— like spaghetti."

Today Mimi was clear and sharp, and her eyes glowed like amethysts. "You look down in the dumps," she said. "Having trouble with the running coach?"

I didn't want to bother Mimi with my problems, so I said, no, everything was fine. "Ms. Llord's still driving me crazy," I added.

Mimi nodded sympathetically and continued to play. "You have to persevere," she told me over the strains of the music. "Don't let the Ms. Llords of life grind you down or your goose is pissed."

It was the first time in days that I'd felt like laughing. "That's better," Mimi said. "Now that you don't look so woebegone, tell me the news. Are your parents still coming home at all hours from that damned store?"

"Are you mad at them?" I blurted.

"For sending me over the hill to the Manse? I was, Meg, I surely was." Mimi's fingers slid into a melody I'd known since I was in diapers—a soft, rippling, melancholy-sweet folk lullaby. I thought Mimi would hum the words as she'd done to me so many times, but instead she spoke in a clear, matter-of-fact voice. "I thought I was dished up when they brought me here. I was sure I'd loathe it. But actually, it's not so bad hanging out with the members of the First-Floor Club."

"Say, what?"

"Residents who live on the first floor," Mimi explained, "like Vera, and Silky, Bea Harriway and Sam Saito. They're interesting people who've fallen on difficult times and landed here at the Manse." She chewed on that thought for a moment and then added darkly, "It's not bad here except for the food. They don't put salt in anything."

I closed my eyes and listened to my grandmother coax the keys into song. As Silky had said, she played like an angel. And if Mimi could hang in, so could I. Somehow I was going to catch those creeps at their dirty work. And then, I swore to myself, I wasn't going to be the one whose goose was pissed.

When I went home, there were a bunch of messages on the garbled answering machine tape—most of them X-rated. I was so mad that when the phone rang, I snatched it up and snarled, "Cut it out, or I'll call the cops."

"Whoa," Jed's voice came back, "back off, it's just me. I guess you've been getting a lot of crank calls?" I said, he might say that. "You think Diana and her buddies are behind this, right?"

"How did you know?"

Jed said that it hadn't been that hard to figure out. "You were asking me about them the other day, and one of the guys on the team told me you had a big blowout with Diana's friends during lunch." He paused. "Did you tell your folks?"

I told him no, because I had no proof. Then I told him what Mrs. Alvarez had said. "It could've happened that way," Jed said, thoughtful and serious. "I remember Rea getting in trouble at middle school and seeing her mother waiting in the office to talk to the principal. Have you ever played the Hunters game at Video Center down by Six Corners?"

While I was trying to catch up with this sudden change

of subject, Jed launched into an explanation of the game. In it you were the good guy running away from a bunch of sadistic killers. According to Jed, it was a pisser game and your chances weren't too good of staying alive. "Once you're dead, the game ends," he added.

Somewhat impatiently, I asked him what this had to do with Diana. "She and the others walked in one time while I was playing Hunters. She watched for a while and I asked her if she wanted to play. She went, why bother with pretend games? Hunts in real life were a lot more interesting. Then she and the others smiled at each other."

Remembering Cass's evil smile, I felt cold all over. The girls wanted amusing prey—real people who bled and suffered like Rea Alvarez, and me. But *why* would they want to torment other kids?

"Maybe they're bored," Jed suggested.

He proceeded to tell me that the Angelis were loaded, that Vi's parents jointly owned a chain of record stores, and that Cass's stepfather was Mr. Moneybags. "One time in algebra class she mentioned that her folks give her everything she wants before she wants it. She said it gets boring after a while," Jed finished.

I thought about my folks working so hard just to keep from going under and Mrs. Alvarez afraid to leave Chisolm because she needed to keep her job. I hated those girls for being rich and bored, but that wasn't going to help. "I've got to get proof that they're doing stuff to me," I told Jed, and he said yeah, he knew.

"Have you finished with my lab notes?" he then asked. This time I took his topic change without batting an eye

121

and said I had. "Bring them to the athletic field tomorrow morning before school," he went. "I have an idea."

Next morning I took my bike so's to get to school early and was waiting at the field when Jed came jogging up. With him was a thin girl I didn't know. "This is Nancy," Jed said.

Nancy had sandy hair and narrow blue eyes that watched me warily as we said hi. "We ran in a couple of meets together back at good old Chisolm Middle School," Jed explained.

"Yeah, but then I got bone spurs." Then, cutting short the small talk, Nancy went, "Jed says you're having trouble with the Hunters."

The Hunters. "You're in for a rough ride," Nancy added when I nodded. "Those are three very cool, slick girls, especially Diana. She is the girl most likely to be elected to anything, the girl teachers love to have in class, the person kids want for their best friend. It's like people are always saying, 'Do you know Diana? She's so *wonderful*.' "

Nancy broke off to roll her eyes at people's stupidity. "Tell her what happened to your friend Mary," Jed prompted.

"Well, Mary was, you know, my neighbor. We didn't hang around together too much because she was kind of boy crazy." Nancy shifted her backpack. "Mary liked a boy that Diana liked, and he sort of liked Mary more than he liked Diana—"

Once again breaking off, she looked around her so uneasily that I felt nervous myself. "What did Diana do?" I questioned.

"She didn't *do* anything, know what I mean? But somehow, word got around that Mary was a slut. Kids

122

were saying it and passing notes about it and stuff. It was really bad—Mary's best friends quit being friends with her. It was like she had some kind of awful disease or something."

Nancy looked around her again. Jed prompted, "Mary thought her boyfriend had started the rumors, right?"

"Yeah. They had this huge fight and broke up. Afterward, the guy started to hang out with Diana."

Nancy shifted her backpack again. "That's the way the Hunters operate, know what I mean? They never do anything up front where people can see them. They do things sneakily, secretly. And they're smart! Nobody ever suspects them or blames them for anything. They dump all over people and walk away smelling like roses."

There was a small silence, during which we could hear the first bell. "Did the, ah, Hunters go after Rea Alvarez?" I asked as we headed toward school.

Nancy just shrugged, so I explained, "Diana's trying to trash me for asking questions about Rea."

"You can't trap the Hunters, they're too smart," Nancy warned. "Look, I told you about Mary because Jed asked me to, but that's all I'm doing. I am *outie*."

She hefted her backpack and took off at a jog. In other words, she didn't even want to be seen with me. Nancy was scared of what Diana could do to her just for talking to me.

"I know most of the kids from Chisolm," Jed offered. "Maybe one of them can tell us something. I'll ask around."

With my eyes on Nancy's retreating back, I said, "Are

123

you sure you want to? The Hunters may go after you, too, Jed."

"Yeah, well, I like to live dangerously." Jed's long-boned face went grim as he added, "Besides, I want to find out what really happened to Rea."

EIGHT

MIMI HAS A favorite saying: what you can't walk around, you have to step over.

For a week the phone kept ringing and guys whistled at me in the corridors. Obscene notes were stuck in my book bag and kids I'd known for years gave me weird looks and lots of air. It was like, see you *later,* Meg.

Was I mad, scared, or frustrated? Most times I was all three. My stomach developed more acid than a chemistry lab, I jumped a mile whenever the phone rang. Most of all, I was petrified that Mr. Prudhomme would get a hold of one of "my" so-called advertisements and throw me off the team.

But he didn't. Instead, when we raced against Dulton High and I ran the three-miler in under twenty minutes, he actually told me I'd done well and hinted about the league meet again. So I ran my lungs out, meanwhile pretending to ignore the whistles, the notes, and the phone calls.

Eventually the hassling slowed down until it stopped completely. This time, though, I wasn't fooled. Diana and her pals were just thinking up their next move. It was like, when you least expect it, Meg, expect it. And while

I was waiting for whatever *it* was to happen, Mimi came home for Sunday dinner.

Mom and I went to fetch her together, both of us nervous and determined not to show it. I clung to Mimi's hand all the ride home, and Mom kept shooting her little looks as if she were going to start foaming at the mouth. But she was beautiful. When Dad came home for dinner, she asked him about the business as if she really cared. Then she praised Mom's cooking and salted it all she wanted, meanwhile telling us about the interesting people she'd met at the home.

Most of the people I already knew, so I just sat back and watched Mom and Dad laugh at Mimi's descriptions and comments about everybody and especially about Silky Sulieman. "He's—well, he *was* a CPA, had a heart attack and a quadruple bypass, which landed him at the Manse," Mimi explained. "Like somebody else I could mention, Silky's joy in life was running. He ran the Boston Marathon for twenty years straight, can you believe it? Now he's another member of the First-Floor Club, in need of temporary assistance until he can join the mainstream again."

She looked straight at Dad, who ducked the challenge. "With all those people you're meeting, Mother," he said, "you must be busy all day."

"I work at it," she shot back. "I'm getting to be quite adept at filling my days, Jerry. If I don't watch out, I may become a workaholic like you and Nolly."

I shifted, uncomfortable at the dry note in her voice, but Mimi then changed the subject and her tone and asked about some new herb tea she'd read about. As she listened and asked interested questions I wanted to stand

126

up and cheer for her. She was one thousand percent better than she'd been.

After dinner, Mimi slid an arm through mine and drew me down into her favorite couch, the one she'd brought with her when she broke up her and Papa Ned's house. "You haven't told me about yourself, Meg," she said. "How's life?" Fine, I said. "And how is that young football fan who came over here with Karen?"

Did Mimi suspect that Kenny and I had a thing going? "I'm not friends with Karen and her new buddies anymore," I explained.

My grandmother looked surprised. "Ninth grade is a time when interests change and people go their separate ways. Still, you and Munch go a long way back together."

"We're just not close anymore," I repeated.

Violet-blue eyes, loving, concerned, lingered on mine. She knew there'd been trouble, but she wasn't going to pry. My insides griped with a misery deeper than anything the Hunters could dump on me. With a terrible loneliness for Mimi that I knew she shared.

"It's no biggie," I told her as nonchalantly as I could. "It happens, you know? And I've got a new lab partner."

I told her about Jed, whereupon Mimi brightened, allowed that Jed sounded like a man to count on, and added that she'd like to meet him. "Bring him around to the Manse soon," she said, and reached out to cup my cheek in her hand.

Featherlight touch, remembered from my babyhood with lullabies and kisses—I wanted to drop my head on Mimi's shoulder and tell her everything that had been happening to me, but I held back. Mimi had her share of troubles without borrowing any of mine.

When it came time to drive back to Meadowriver, I couldn't face it. Fetching her home was one thing—driving her back to the nursing home and *leaving* her there was something else. So I offered to wash the dishes and, kissing Mimi by the door, waved her off and cranked up my new Stone Temple Pilots CD full blast. Then, when that didn't work, I put on my sweats and running shoes and took off for a run. Sweat, I figured, might drown out loneliness.

Twilight was deepening into dusk as I stretched out. I ran quickly down our street and, hooking a left on wood-shadowed Fern Way, turned onto Mountain Road. At first the wind was cold through my jacket, but as I picked up speed it felt good. Nobody was out this Sunday evening, so I had the winding road to myself, and I was focusing, really getting into my running, when I heard a car engine humming some distance behind me. Turning to look over my shoulder, I saw the far-off glint of headlights.

Mountain Road was really narrow at this point, so I hugged the side of the road. For a while the headlights kept getting nearer and nearer—and then, suddenly, the road went dark.

Had the car stopped? I whipped a glance over my shoulder just in time to see a huge mass of darkness moving up on me, fast. As the lightless car whooshed past me someone gave this loud yell.

I was so startled I stumbled and nearly fell over. Then hoots of laughter from the still-darkened car made indignation replace my shock. "Jerk!" I yelped. "Are you crazy?"

128

As if he'd heard, the driver slammed on the brakes. The car came to a screeching, rocking stop just ahead of me and then started backing up.

Really scared now, I swiveled around and started to run. As I sprinted I heard a muffled male voice croon, "He-ey, party girl, want some fun?"

The voice, the car, were almost on top of me. Heart pounding against my rib cage, I ran into the trees that edged the road. Behind me, I could hear laughter. "Don't try to hide, sweet cheeks!" the mocking male voice called.

The voice sounded hoarse and muffled, as if whoever it was had covered his mouth with something. Maybe he was masked, I thought.

"Par-ty gi-irl!"

Now there were *two* voices crooning. Two—or more—guys were after me. Scared to death, I ran on. I was sure that any second I'd hear the sound of pursuing feet, that arms would lunge out to grab me.

I don't know how long I ran. How far into the woods. I just know that my breath was one painful wheeze and my heart was pounding as if it was getting ready to burst. Then I stopped because I couldn't run anymore, stopped and listened—listened to silence.

And I do mean, silence. There was no sound. Nothing. Just the sough of the wind through the trees and the sound of autumn insects. He—they—whoever it was had gone. I'd outrun them. I was safe.

Then someone began to laugh in the shadows.

Breath caught in my ribs, and I stood there, gulping air and straining my ears for that soft, evil, taunting sound. It came again. Close. *Very* close.

I tried to run again, but my legs felt wobbly, and I couldn't move. "Get away from me," I tried to scream, but the words wouldn't even form in my throat.

For the third time the night picked up and echoed the sound of spiteful laughter, and this time my vocal cords worked. "Get away from me!" I yelled.

Clumsily, I jolted forward. Or tried to. My toe connected with a root or a rock, pain shot through my foot and leg, and I fell forward onto my knees.

I knew they'd be right behind me. Knew I should try to get up and run. Couldn't. Had no breath, no strength left. Heard myself whimper with fear—

But that broken whimper was the only sound I heard. There was no more laughter. Nothing. Except for the insects and the wind, it seemed that I was alone in the world.

Shaking in every part of my body, I hoisted myself to my feet and made my way back to the road. When I looked up, a pale sickle moon rode the clouds. The moon of Diana the Huntress.

Scratched and bruised and scared to death, I made it home as quick as I could. I wanted my folks to call the police and *get* those guys, but when I burst into the house, Mom and Dad weren't home. The house was silent, empty except for Gorki, who took one look at me and backed away, muttering and making growl sounds under her breath.

I ran around the house slamming and locking doors and windows, and even then I felt scared. Now what? I asked myself. Now what, Meg?

Now I could phone Mom and Dad at Meadowriver and beg them to get home and call the police. But the staff person I spoke to at the facility told me my folks had just left. I next thought of Jed, but his phone was busy.

Gorki finally came near me, so I picked her up and held her tightly just so's to have something warm to hang on to. "Okay," I told her as she struggled to free herself, "it's okay. I'll wait till they come home."

But waiting made me realize that telling my folks wouldn't get me anywhere. Had I got a license-plate number or even seen the make of the car? No. Had I recognized either of the male voices? No. And the laughter I'd heard could've been male or female—

The phone shrilled so loud that I squashed Gorki, who scratched me and took off, tail fluffed out to red alert. I stared at the ringing phone. If I heard that mocking laughter again, I knew I'd fall apart.

But it was only Jed, and when I heard his voice, I wanted to cry in pure relief. And like tears, the words came bursting out of me. "Diana's warning me," I babbled.

It would have been the kind of game Diana'd play— scaring me into running like a crazy person through the woods. Never touching me, never really openly threatening me, just letting my own fear act like a cattle prod. And I'd played her game. I'd acted like a scared, hunted animal for her amusement.

Anger melted away some of my fear as I figured it all out. Diana *wanted* me to go to the police. She was waiting for me to look foolish by making accusations I couldn't prove. "Not this girl," I swore. "Now I know Diana's worried I'm getting close to the truth about her and the Hunters—"

"You're the one who should be worried," Jed interrupted. "This is getting too rough, Meg. I think you

131

need to tell your parents about what happened tonight. I would."

I told Jed that I couldn't tell my folks for the same reason I couldn't go to the police. It'd just worry them. What could they do except forbid me to ever run alone again, or ride my bike anywhere, alone? A lot of good that'd do.

Jed was silent for a moment. Then he burst out, "The slimebuckets in the car have to be Kenny Draper and B. K. Simmons. The word is that Kenny's so into Diana, he'd do anything for her, and B.K. sits on his brains." Angrily he added, "I wish you could have recognized the jerks' voices."

So next day, I listened to voices around school and played a guessing game. Was it Kenny and/or B.K.? Maybe. Or maybe it was some other guy who liked one of the Hunters. I felt so sick of the possibilities that I didn't want to think about it anymore.

I didn't see Jed that day except at biology, but when I got out of practice, he was waiting for me. "You said you might be visiting your grandmother last night, so I figured I might as well bike along with you to Meadowriver," he said offhandedly.

I told Jed he didn't have to worry, that those yahoos wouldn't try anything in broad daylight, but all the time I was talking, I was really relieved that Jed was coming with me. Though I would never have admitted it, my riding my bike to school had been a defiant gesture that I'd already started to regret.

"Don't you have to get home?" I felt I had to say.

"I checked with Ma—she's cool with it," Jed said, adding, "We can take Spruce Way."

Spruce Way was a narrow, hilly, hardly traveled dirt road great for bikers or runners, and best of all it was a shortcut to the nursing home. Soon we were at Meadow-river, where we were greeted by trails of music drifting through the lobby.

"Is that your grandmother?" Jed asked, impressed, as we followed the music down the hall. "What's that she's playing?"

Mimi was giving a rousing version of one of her all-time favorites, "Some Enchanted Evening" from *South Pacific*. Apparently it was a lot of other people's favorite, too, because today the recreation room was really jumping. A lot of seniors had circled the piano, and everybody was singing or croaking or wheezing along.

"She's great," Jed shouted in my ear, and I felt this huge sense of pride. I knew how hard it'd been for Mimi to come to a home, how hard to adjust. But she was making it. No way was she going gentle into anybody's good night.

And I wasn't beaten yet; no, ma'am! I pushed up my chin and straightened my back as the last chords of the song washed over the room. Then there was silence and Ms. Pors boomed, "Goodness, lamb, that takes me *way* back. I recall that I was with my late husband then—Frank was such a romantic soul. Used to hold my hand and tell me I was *way* prettier than Mary Martin."

She wiped her eyes with the back of her hand and faded little Miss Harriway sighed and whispered that she and her dear sister had gone to see the show years ago. Others began to tell *their* stories, and Mimi nodded and beamed, her fingers trailing gently over the keys. Then she spotted us by the door.

"Meg!" she called.

Mimi's fans were used to seeing me around by now, and we approached to a chorus of greetings from the First-Floor Club. "Who's the boyfriend?" Silky wanted to know.

He plodded his walker forward, holding out his bone-crushing paw first to me and then to Jed. "You've got the look of a distance runner, too," he told Jed, when I introduced them. Then, blue eyes glinting like bits of autumn sky, he told us about the last marathon he'd run.

Silky's body might have gotten scrawny, his legs might have failed him, but his strong, clear voice guided Jed and me through the streets of Boston and up the solid wall of Heartbreak Hill. "Oy, that hill—it was something else," he recalled. "My old friend, that hill was, and also my nemesis. Someday you two kids will run up that hill, and you'll give it my compliments, am I right? Tell it Silky said hello."

Then he asked about our running, and enthusiastically Jed talked about the state meet. "If I can make it to the league meet, I'll have a chance," he said eagerly. "I'm trying to run the two-miler under nine twenty-eight."

"My money's on you." Silky shook hands again. "You enjoy your visit, now, and I'll catch you young people later."

"Silky's a nice man," I said as he plodded off.

"So he is." Mimi's smile broadened into a grin, which she transferred to Jed. "I'm glad to know you, Jed Berringer."

Jed shook Mimi's outstretched hand gently and asked, "How are you today, Mrs. Castleway?" to which she said that she was Mimi to everyone who counted.

Mimi was in really good form today. She played for us and coaxed me into trying the Paganini again. Then, saying I'd made a lot of progress, she told us hilarious stories about her days as a music teacher. We got to laughing so hard that I actually forgot where we were until Ruth Winton dropped by to tell Mimi she really loved *South Pacific*.

"Ruth is very good at what she does," my grandmother commented as the head day nurse went on her way. "Kind but not patronizing. Present but not hovering."

"You like it here, Mimi." It was a statement, a question, a plea—take your pick. She paused and looked up at me, her eyes direct as they'd ever been.

"I want to come home," she said.

I held my breath. Mimi had said those words over and over during the first, confused days after she'd moved to Meadowriver. Then, later, she hadn't spoken about coming home anymore. Last night over dinner she'd hinted at it to Dad, but she hadn't been so direct.

"I feel like myself again," Mimi went on. "As I say, the staff here knows its stuff. The medication I'm on is wonderful—very few cobwebs in the brain box, these days. I think I can function in a family setting again." She turned to Jed. "What do you think?"

"You'd get my vote," he said, meaning it. "I think you'd do excellent."

Mimi patted Jed's hand and turned to me. "Well, Meg? Want to be my advocate with your parents?"

Around two huge lumps in the throat, I told her that she knew I would. "I've missed you," I whispered.

135

"Likewise. Well," Mimi added briskly, "we might as well face facts. I imagine they'll keep me here for some more time before they spring me, but if I have my way, I'll be home with you by Thanksgiving. All right?"

It made me feel so happy that tears filled my eyes. I held up a hand, and she high-fived it. "Sa' *right*!"

"Good. Now, last night you looked as if you wanted to talk about something that was really troubling you. What is it?"

Startled by her change of subject, a shift as abrupt as Jed's ever were, I suddenly felt it all again—the fear, the feel of branches whipping my face, the laughter. "It'll work itself out," I said. "Like you always say, if you can't step around it—"

"Don't quote me to my face," Mimi retorted. "Things must be really bad." I said nothing. "Has it something to do with—I seem to recall that a classmate of yours killed herself."

"Really, it's nothing to worry about, Mimi. I'm handling it."

She frowned thoughtfully. "Meaning you don't want to worry me with your problems. Have you talked to your parents?" I shook my head. "Why not? They need to know what's happening to you."

"I think so, too," Jed cut in before I could hush him, "but Meg wants to wait until we can find some answers about how Rea died."

I scowled Jed quiet and told Mimi not to worry and to please not say a word to the folks. She seemed to process this for a long moment and then said, "Chip away at your problem, then. Keep at it till you find the truth."

136

My grandmother leaned over to rest her long, strong fingers gently on my arm. "Truth," she declared, "is what shames the devil."

Jed was impressed with Mimi. "I should write about her for English." I looked a question at him and he explained, "It's this dumb assignment. We have to write about a notable living person, and your grandma's about as notable as they make them."

Next time we visited Meadowriver together—both of us running across Spruce Way this time—he asked her if she'd mind his writing about her. Mimi was tickled pink. "Did you plan to interview me?" she asked, but Jed said no, it was going to be informal.

"Would you like to see it before I hand it in?" he asked, and Mimi said it wasn't necessary; she trusted him.

I was glad that Jed and Mimi were getting along so well. I'd never have admitted it to anyone, but since that evening, I'd been uneasy about running alone on lonely roads. Jed's liking Mimi and writing about her meant he'd come with me to visit her after school.

Most times, after a long visit with Mimi, me and Jed would run up to the Berringer house. I got to know his folks that way, and I liked them. Mr. Berringer worked for the post office and was a quiet, gentle guy who grew orchids in his own little greenhouse. Mrs. B was just the opposite, a dynamo who whizzed between selling real estate and a dozen and a half church and town committees. Even so, she always had time to sit down and talk with us, to ask after Mimi, and even to send her cookies she'd baked herself—though most of them were a little burned.

Since Mr. or Mrs. B always drove me home, I could go

and see Mimi without worrying about being ambushed. This meant that I could concentrate on improving my speed during those runs to Meadowriver. I couldn't touch Jed's speed, but he sure gave me something to shoot for. On those afternoons I could push away all other bothersome thoughts in my head and focus only on running.

So we ran through September and into October's first golden days. Meanwhile at school, I waited for the Hunters to make their next move. Nothing happened, except that Darryl Haas got his second F in biology and Diana was nominated for student council. Signs with HAVE AN ANGEL WORKING FOR YOU AS FRESHMEN REP and GO, ANGELI! sprouted all along the corridor.

On my way to fifth-period study one day, I found Karen taping another sign near my locker. "Think you have a chance?" I asked.

It was the first time I'd spoken to Karen in weeks. At first I didn't think she was going to answer, but then she went, "We're gonna win."

She sounded so smug that I couldn't help needling her. "You're sure about that? Diana'd better watch out. She's got a lot of competition."

"Oh, we're gonna win. We're gonna get it." Karen's tone took on an almost chantlike quality before she stopped to give me a dirty look. "You're the one who should watch out."

I came right back, "Oh, I do. With your little clique on the prowl, I definitely watch my back."

A few kids, passing us en route to class, gave us curious looks. "It's your fault," Munch said. She'd got all red, and her eyes were snapping. "You could have had it all. You could've been *in*—"

She broke off, grabbed up her tape and roll of posters, and took off. "No thanks," I told her retreating back. "I wouldn't have been one of Diana's little helpers for anything."

I went to study in a real down mood. I wasn't as much worried about what the girls would do to me as bothered that Munch had changed so much. I was still glooming about this when the girl beside me passed me a note.

It read, *I used to date Cass. If you want to talk about it, meet me after school in back of the gym. Alone. Don't tell anyone, or I won't show.*

The note wasn't signed. I looked questioningly at the girl who'd passed me the note, and she pointed to the back of the room. I scoped the guys who were sitting in back, but no one even looked my way.

An anonymous note—it was a trap, right? Had to be. That stuff about coming alone and not telling anyone had been lifted straight out of one of the cop shows on TV. I'd be a fool to go along with what this guy said, I decided. I'd tell Jed about the note during math.

But I didn't. I sat through the class without hearing a word and, at the end of it, told Jed an elaborate excuse why I wasn't going to see Mimi that day after practice. Then, when Jed had taken off to run by himself, I looped around to the back of the gym to see if the guy who wrote the note would show.

No one was there. Of course not, I told myself. Grow up, Meg. It was just a trick to see how fast you'd gobble down the bait—

"Ah, Meg?" a voice went behind me.

I whipped around to see a dark-haired guy my age. He was about as tall as Jed but chunkier, and had a pretty good build. Not bad, I thought, in fact, good-looking, though not my type. He was probably the kind of baby-jock that Cass would have wanted to date in eighth grade.

"Did you send me that note?" I asked warily.

He had. His name was Wes Peterson, and he'd dated Cass last year for about a month. "I overheard you talking to that girl near the lockers," he told me. "I think you might want to know some stuff."

Experience had made me careful. "Depends on what kind of stuff we're talking about," I parried. "You say you and Cass went out?"

He nodded. "In eighth grade. Man, it was like dating three girls because Cass and Diana and Vi were so tight. It was kind of spooky how close they were. You know— they'd be giggling and talking and the moment I came in the room it was, like, silence. Then one time I went over to Diana's house—"

Wes Peterson broke off. After I'd prodded him along, he said, "Look, maybe I shouldn't tell you any of this."

"Suit yourself," I said. "I'll see you around."

No, he said, wait, he'd tell me. "You've been to Diana's house?" I nodded. "You know that big portrait of Mrs. Angeli all dressed up in that nightgown thing?" I nodded again. "Diana likes to dress up like that, too."

All the while he was telling me this he kept glancing around us and over his shoulder. Nervous myself, I listened impatiently as Wes told me that one time Cass had broken a date with him because she had an upset stomach.

"We were supposed to get a pizza after school. No biggie. Except that evening, I realized I'd taken her English notebook home in my backpack, and we had a major quiz next day."

Wes had called her house, found out she was at Diana's. "We live a few blocks from the Angelis," he went on, "so I went over. The parents' Mercedes was gone, the door was unlocked, so I went inside."

Wes gulped and kicked the grass at his feet. "What happened?" I prompted.

"There were voices coming from the living room, so I went there. The door was almost shut, but"— Wes's Adam's apple bobbed again in a gulp—"I could see the girls inside. All of them had on these see-through night-gown things, and Diana had a silver band around her forehead with a crescent moon on it. They were going, 'We are the hunters of the night.' "

So the Hunters liked to dress up. With uniforms, yet. What nice girls' club doesn't? But my sarcastic thought drifted away as Wes went, "And they were sort of chanting, 'We're gonna get her, yeah, gonna get that Rea.' "

We're gonna win. We're gonna do it.

I reached out and grabbed his arm. "You're sure they said *Rea*?" He nodded unhappily. "What else?"

"She—Diana—said something about Rea's mother asking for trouble by daring to go to the principal and that Rea didn't know what trouble meant. Then she giggles, and goes, 'Now we'll take our blood oath to the moon goddess like we always do,' and Cass picks up this plate with this *gross* raw blob of meat on it, it looked like liver or something totally gross, man, and they all cut off a piece and *ate* it—"

He broke off, looking sick and shaking his head. "It was, like, totally insane. I was *outie,* man. I didn't want anything more to do with that kind of stuff." I asked, did he break up with Cass, and he gave me a look that said, Was I crazy, or what?

"But you never told anyone about what you saw. You never said anything when Rea was in trouble," I accused.

"I felt really bad about that, but what could I do? I didn't have any proof. Like, if I'd had a camera, or a tape recorder, or anything. Besides, those girls are totally *messed*—"

He broke off, and I knew what he was thinking. To relate a lame story like that about three good little girls— it'd be his word against theirs. And if they found out he'd seen them, they might be after *him.*

"So why tell me now?" I asked.

"I know that, ah, stuff's been happening to you." Once again Wes checked over his shoulder before adding, "When I saw you talking to that girl. Be *careful,* man."

I admit to looking over my shoulder a few times myself while I was biking home that day. What Cass's old boyfriend had told me gave me the creeps. Once home, I locked the front door, went upstairs to Mimi's room, and took down her leather-bound book about Greek and Roman myths.

And there, on page 102, was a whole chapter about the moon goddess. As Mimi had said, Diana was a cruel goddess. She killed people who spied on her sacred rituals, and she and her followers hunted their victims to the death. I turned a page and saw a painting of Diana in her see-through huntress's costume with a crescent moon riding on her fair hair.

142

We're gonna get that Rea—

I shut the book with trembling hands. "I have to get proof," I muttered.

Next day, when I told Jed, he first yelled at me for not telling him about the note, and then said that this was getting really weird. "The guy's right—nobody is going to believe that stuff without evidence," he said gloomily. "Better watch yourself."

As if I didn't know enough to do that. I checked out my shadow twice before even leaving the house, double-locked my locker—but nothing happened. Nothing except that with Jed's help, I managed to get a B+ on one of Ms. Llord's awful biology tests.

That was Friday. To celebrate, I asked Mom if I could invite Jed to Sunday dinner when Mimi was home. Little did I know what I was unleashing on the Fairlings. For someone who was as skinny as he was, Jed put away a *lot* of food, and even after three huge helpings of roast chicken, stuffing, corn, potatoes, and biscuits, he still looked hungry.

"I like a man with a healthy appetite," Mimi said as I stared at Jed in amazement. "Silky eats the same way. Must be something runners do."

Mom suggested that Silky might like a piece of apricot pie. "I'll bet he would," Mimi went, looking pleased. "And a bit of that chicken, Nolly, if you can spare it. You have no idea how awful unsalted food can be."

It was a fun evening. Mimi played the piano, and even Dad sang. Then we took a walk together, and it made me feel warm to the tips of my toes to see how Mimi marched along with her shoulders pushed back. Then, after we'd dropped Jed at the Berringers', the rest of us escorted Mimi back to Meadowriver together.

"Ah," Dad went, "what do we have here? Looks like a welcoming committee, Mother."

Silky Sulieman was hovering near the door, all dressed up in shirt and tie and with a carnation attached to his walker. His million wrinkles all dissolved into a huge smile when Mimi introduced him to the folks.

"The family of a musical angel has got to be special, am I right?" Silky thanked Mom for the pie and then turned to Mimi. "If you're ready, Ms. Castleway, your audience's waiting in the rec room."

Mimi took his proffered arm and they walked off. Dad laughed. "How *about* that," he said. "The old girl has a gentleman admirer. How about *that*."

He sounded happier than I'd heard him in a long time. "She seems like her old self," Mom said. Her eyes were shining. "Maybe it will work out that she can come home to live with us again. She seems so much more stable and rational. Don't you think so, Jerry?"

My dad nodded. "If she keeps up like this, there'd be no problem," he said. Then, remembering to be reasonable, he added, "But we have to be careful. She may be making this much progress because she's at Meadowriver. We have to wait and see for her sake as well as ours, Nolly, all right?"

Sa' right, Mimi!

I went to bed happy that night and woke up happy. I whistled to myself as I went to school. At homeroom, the kids from the school newspaper came by, and I bought a copy and thumbed through it while waiting for English class to start. "How about that," I exclaimed.

144

The paper had printed some of those "notable living character" sketches that Jed was talking about. I ran my eye down the list of sketches, chuckled as I saw one about Ms. Llord, then stopped at Jed's name. His title was: "The Old Lady Who Plays the Piano."

I read it quickly, eager to see what Jed had written about Mimi, expecting to be pleased. But though the article started by describing an old woman with eyes "almost like Elizabeth Taylor," it quickly went sour.

Disbelieving, I read about Mimi's "restless fingers" moving over the keys of a piano "even when there's no piano in front of her." Then came the worst: a description of a brain-dead old lady losing her way and wandering around in circles until the police came to get her.

It was pathetic. It was awful. It was all the more cruel because it could've only been written by someone who knew her. "No," I told myself, "Jed wouldn't have done this."

How do you know? a nasty little voice whispered in my mind. I'd told Jed a lot of stuff about Mimi. Maybe he'd written it for English class in a hurry, sent it in, and never believed in a million years that his cruel caricature would be published. Maybe that was how it happened.

Next class was Ms. Llord's. I practically ran there and found Jed waiting for me. "It wasn't me," he declared before I could speak. "I never wrote that crap."

He reached into his notebook and pulled out a piece of paper that had an A on it. It was titled, "The Lady Who Plays Memories."

Quickly I scanned it. It was an affectionate, funny sketch about Mimi playing for the old folks, who remembered their past as they listened to her music. Reading the

145

words, I could hear Jed talking and felt almost sick with relief.

Jed had nothing to do with the cruel sketch in the paper, but I knew who did. "They wrote it," I muttered.

They. The Hunters. The followers of the moon goddess—Diana, Vi, Cass, and Karen.

They had done this because they knew Jed was my friend, my ally. They'd wanted to ruin our friendship and leave me isolated. "But as usual," Jed said, "you'll never prove it. If you ask the editors of the paper, they'll just say they found this thing submitted with the others. Nobody will claim it."

Just then I heard Diana's voice in the hall outside. She and Vi were strolling past the classroom door. Diana was laughing, and the sound of it made something inside me snap. I ran out of the classroom, darted across the hallway, and planted myself in front of Diana. "I know what you did," I snarled.

She looked at me as if I were some bug in her path. "Excuse me?" she asked coldly.

"Don't play Ms. Innocent," I cried. "I guess you got Karen to help you describe my grandmother, and I suppose you pulled a few strings to get your 'masterpiece' published under Jed's name. You want to break up our friendship, don't you? Well, it didn't work."

Diana rolled her eyes. "I think you're sick," she said, in a pitying tone. "I'd be mad at you, but I can't be mad at somebody who's as messed in the head as you are."

"You're the one who's sick," I raged.

"Meg, back off." Jed had followed me into the hall. He grabbed my arm, but I shook him off. "Meg, *chill*."

146

People in the hall were turning to stare at us. Diana smiled at Jed and said, "Nice article, Jed."

"Like I wrote it," Jed retorted, getting red in the face himself. Diana just smiled. "You know who did write it, don't you, Diana?"

"I don't know what you're talking about."

Coolly, she flipped back her long hair and started to walk away. I grabbed her shoulder and spun her around. "Don't you *dare* walk away from me," I cried.

"Let go of her," Vi threatened. The drawl was completely gone, and her made-up eyes were hard as rock. "If you want trouble, Fairling, you'll get it."

"And don't threaten me, either." Vi's nostrils flared as I added, "You think you're so smart that you'll get away with all the things you do, but you won't. I swear I'll find out a way to get you."

I tore the newspaper up and threw the pieces in Diana's face. For a second her eyes narrowed. Then she sighed and said, "I feel *so* sorry for you, Meg."

Before I could react to this, Ms. Llord spoke at my shoulder. "Meg, get to class at once."

"But," I stammered, "she—"

"At once," Lord Doom repeated. "You, too, Jed. I thought you were too levelheaded to be caught up in a brawl."

"It's not a brawl," I protested. "You don't know what Diana did. She—"

"The class bell has rung," Ms. Llord interrupted again. "Both you and Jed will have detention with me today. And pick up the mess you've made," she added, pointing at the scraps of newspaper on the ground.

I looked over my shoulder, but Diana and Vi had gone. As I grabbed up the torn bits of newspaper, I knew that

147

I'd played into the Hunters' hands. Once again I'd lost my cool and come on like a witch while they themselves walked away smelling like roses.

NINE

WHILE I WAS in social studies the office intercom demanded that I march myself down to the office, and when I got there, our principal was waiting for me.

"I heard that you threatened another student with bodily harm," he began.

Had Ms. Llord ratted on me? But no— "Mrs. Angeli just telephoned me," Mr. MacMasters was going on. "She heard what happened this morning and was concerned for her daughter's safety."

Little Diana had lost no time running to Mommy. Too scared of MacMasters to dwell on *that* irony, I started to explain what had happened, but no sale. "I'm talking to you as a warning," our principal went.

Eyes glued to my face, he added, "I give one warning and one warning only, Meg. Your name's been cropping up a lot these days, and I've heard disturbing things about you. Is this yours?"

He flipped a Meg-the-party-girl index card across his desk at me. "No," I cried. "I never wrote that. Diana or her friends did."

"That's a serious accusation," MacMasters said. "Do you have proof?" Miserable and angry, I could only shake my head. "I think I understand," he went on. "Diana Angeli is a good student and popular with the other students. Her teachers think she's a great kid. She's a candidate for the freshman student council. It's understandable that you're jealous—"

"It's not *like* that!"

"But being jealous doesn't give you the right to threaten her or try to get her in trouble," Mr. MacMasters finished as if I hadn't spoken.

He leaned forward across his desk and leveled an accusing finger at me. "I identify the troublemakers in my building, Meg. I know who you are. If you try to cause any more trouble in *my* school, you will be *sorry*."

Then he finally let me go, upon which I ran to the lav and threw up. By now I had a wicked headache, and by lunchtime I was totally miserable with it. I didn't think I could face lunch, but because Jed was waiting for me, I made myself go down to the cafeteria.

Bad mistake. Over our so-called lunch, Jed read me the riot act for losing it and tearing into Diana. "She made *you* look bad, not her," he accused. "And now we both have detention with Ms. Llord, and I'll probably be late for practice."

My pointing out that I was in the same boat didn't calm Jed down. According to him, even the smallest of pea brains would have seen that getting mad was what Diana wanted me to do. "You say you want to catch her at her dirty game, and then you as good as walk right up to her, bend over, and say, 'Please kick me.' "

I'd been kicking *myself* for my stupidity all morning, and Jed's remarks sure didn't help. I told him so, and we snap-snarled at each other for a few minutes until Jed got up from the table and stalked off, mad.

Too proud to call him back and apologize, too dispirited to care that my running was so awful that Prudhomme tore me apart during practice, I finally made it home, where a garbled phone message from Mom was waiting. There'd been a problem at the store and the folks wouldn't come home till late. "Make yourself something to eat, honey," Mom's apologetic voice said. "We'll have a bite at the store."

So, what else was new? "You're never here when I need you," I shouted at the message taker. Gorki opened her eyes, startled, whiskers bristling. I snatched her up and buried my face in her soft fur, but she hissed at me and, wriggling out of my arms, hid under the couch. "Oh, go ahead," I yelled at her, "be like everybody else."

I kicked at the magazine rack, which tipped over, spewing mags and newspapers all across the living room. Then, turning my back on the mess, I stomped up the stairs and started to storm past Mimi's empty room. Started to—and then stopped.

Only one person could've told the Hunters all those details about Mimi. Only one person could have supplied ammunition for that rotten article in the SR *Eagle*. I went into my room, snatched up the phone, and punched out Karen's number.

Wonder of wonders, the line was free. "You did it," I shouted, when she answered.

"Who *is* this?" she went, like she didn't know my voice after all these years. "What are you bitching about *now*?"

The rage that had made me grab Diana in the school corridor flared up again. "Like you don't know why I'm

151

calling," I yelled into the phone. "You told Diana all that garbage about Mimi, didn't you?"

Karen hung up the phone.

I dialed her again, and the line rang busy. She was already reporting to the Hunters—but then, Karen was now a Hunter, too. Did she play their little games? I wondered. Did she put on a nightgown and eat raw meat and promise sacrifices to the moon goddess?

If it hadn't been so awful, it'd have been funny. You know, like a Creature Feature rerun of *Vampire Women Strike Again*. But there was really nothing funny about the Hunters. As Mrs. Alvarez said, they were cunning and evil, and getting them riled at me had not been a good idea.

I tried to settle into my homework. Couldn't. The house held silence that was almost physically heavy, and the hours passed, crossed dinnertime without me being hungry. I'd finally gone downstairs to fix myself something when a car swung into the driveway.

The folks were home. My early irritation at them forgotten, I went to the door to call a greeting. "Hard day?" I asked Dad.

"You could say that," he came right back. "Bad enough that business is lousy—I have to get calls complaining about your behavior."

"*My* behavior?"

"Someone called Mr. Julius Angeli telephoned," Dad continued, "and informed me that you'd attacked his daughter at school."

"It's probably some foolish little squabble." Mom had followed Dad up the driveway. "Jerry, don't get so excited."

"I'm not excited," Dad fumed. He strode past me into

152

the house, then turned back to warn, "Don't *ever* let me hear of your raising a hand to anyone again."

"Don't you even want to know what happened?" I cried, but he just kept walking toward the stairs. "You're so unfair," I shouted at his back.

Dad stopped, turned deliberately, and in a cold, hard voice demanded to know whether or not I'd grabbed Diana Angeli in the school hall. "Did you or didn't you threaten her?" he demanded.

"That was because—"

Dad massaged his forehead and his thinning hair. He looked tired and mad at the same time. "Do you want her father to get a restraining order on you, is that it?" he grated. "If I ever hear of you going near that girl, Meg, I'll ground you for a year."

Then he stomped up the stairs. Mom stood twisting her hands worriedly. "Mr. Angeli was awfully upset," she told me. I said, well, I was upset, too, and would she even try to listen instead of yelling at me like I'd murdered someone? "I'm not yelling," Mom started to yell, stopped, and added in a resigned voice, "All right, then. I'm listening."

"Karen told Diana about Mimi," I began.

"That's another thing. Mrs. Tierney came by the store to see me," Mom interrupted. "She said you'd called to say awful things to Karen. Did you?" I said nothing. "Meg, what's got *into* you?"

"Karen wrote an awful article about Mimi and signed Jed's name," I protested. "She did it because Diana told her to. She and her friends do awful things, Mom. They made Rea's life miserable, and now—"

Mom interrupted, "Meg, I can understand why you dislike this Diana Angeli. I know how hard it was to have

153

Munch desert you and become best friends with someone else."

Did Mom think that all this was about *jealousy*? "I know you're in a brand-new school," she went on, "and adjusting to it is difficult, too. Then there's the shock of Mimi's having to go to Meadowriver. It's a lot of pressure on you, but that doesn't mean you can act out like this."

"I'm not—"

"Mrs. Tierney showed me that awful article in the school paper. All I can say is that Jed Berringer is not welcome in this house. But to blame Karen, whom you've known all your life—that's crazy, Meg."

"Jed didn't write that *thing*. They did. Damn it, why can't you listen?" I yelled. Then Dad came to the top of the stairs and bellowed that if I didn't have any respect for my mother, I should go to my room and stay there. And I said, fine, and thanks a lot for their support, after which I slammed into my room, threw myself on the bed, and cried.

Anger pulsed through the house, and with it came hurt and a bitter knowledge that, yes, folks, once again, Diana had won, hands down. She'd set me up, set me up but good, and once again stupid Meg had danced to her tune.

I cried myself to sleep and woke to the drumming of rain. Rain can sound soothing and kind of cool at night when you're snuggled under warm covers—it can be a royal pain in the morning when you have to wait for a bus that's late and the wind blows your umbrella out of your hands. I got soaked, but Karen didn't even show at the bus stop because the Hunters were doubtless being chauffeured to school by Kenny Draper.

154

The thought of Kenny and Karen and the Hunters contributed to a feeling of all-around bummed-outness that resulted in my forgetting my book bag in homeroom. I was out of luck for my first class, and second period I had a biology quiz I couldn't be late for. By the time I finally made it to homeroom to recover the book bag, I was told it'd been sent down to the office.

Naturally, going down to the office made me late for social studies. I zipped into my seat, praying that Mr. Jacobs hadn't seen me, but as clueless as he usually was, this time he'd spotted me sneaking in the door after the bell. "Meg Fairling," he went, "where's your late pass?"

Since he'd gotten that awful note that he believed had come from me, Mr. Jacobs had mostly ignored me. Now I explained about my book bag, and he said nastily, "Well, you'll have to go and get a late pass next period and bring it to me before you go to your next class. Otherwise you won't get credit for your open-book quiz."

Snickers ran through the class. Doris Leo snuffled loudest, probably trying to get on Jacobs's good side. Hating him, I started to open my book bag, but the zipper was stuck.

"What's the difficulty, Meg?" Jacobs demanded.

I gave the zipper a yank and the book bag flapped open. Then both Mr. Jacobs and I stared at this huge knife that lay on top of my books.

"Oh my God," Mr. Jacobs gobbled. "Oh my *God*."

Too stunned to say a word, I continued to stare at the knife. "Stay where you are," Mr. Jacobs hissed at me. "Don't you dare move out of that chair."

"It's not my knife," I finally managed to stammer.

"Then what is it doing in your book bag?" Mr. Jacobs's high voice went into hyperdrive as he added, "You are in *big* trouble, young lady."

"But it's not my knife," I repeated frantically.

Never taking his eyes off me, Mr. Jacobs backed toward the intercom. His face was almost crimson, and his eyes were bugging out of his head. "Don't move," he screeched. "Everybody back in his or her seat. Now!"

Nobody paid any attention. All the kids were on their feet staring at the knife with its cruel, polished blade. "She threatened Diana yesterday," Doris snuffled. "I saw her do it. She told Diana that she'd get her." Pleased that everyone, including Mr. Jacobs, was drinking in every word she said, Doris added importantly, "Diana told me in class that she was scared of what Meg would do."

Mr. Jacobs slammed his hand onto the intercom button and yelled to get the principal up here, *now*. "I have a *situation* here," he yelped.

Almost in tears, I was stammering that I'd never seen the knife before when Mr. MacMasters came bursting in followed by another male teacher. "This will *not* happen in my school," MacMasters said when Mr. Jacobs had shrilled out an explanation. He grabbed my book bag and pointed a finger at me. "You," he grated, "come with me."

As I followed the principal to his office I had a sense that invisible eyes were tracking my progress. Hidden from view, the Hunters were laughing like hyenas.

They'd have laughed even harder if they heard me trying to explain to MacMasters in his office. "You have

156

just broken the laws of the Commonwealth of Massachusetts," he said. "Sit down. I'm calling the police."

He also phoned the store and spoke to my dad. While he was doing that I had a vivid memory of how Dad had looked at me last night. Then, on the heels of that awful thought, I glanced out of the window and saw the flash of red-and-blue lights approaching.

The last time a prowl car had come to school, they'd found drugs in Rea's locker. I blurted, "Diana and Vi and Cass. *They* put the knife in my bag."

"Still trying to blame Diana Angeli for what you did." Mr. MacMasters shot an outraged look at my book bag lying open on his desk. "I told you what would happen if you tried making trouble in this school."

There were voices outside the principal's office, and two police officers came in. One was Officer Oakes, who'd come to our house the day after Rea's suicide. Her eyebrows rose when she recognized me, but before she could say anything, Dad came striding in.

What remained of Dad's hair was messed from hurry, and he looked wound tight with worry. He gave the room a swift once-over, zeroed in on my white face. "Are you okay, Meg?" he cried. "What's going on here?"

Without giving me time to answer, MacMasters told him about the knife. "That's insane," Dad exploded.

"I *didn't* bring it," I wailed. "I never saw the knife before. Really, Dad, I didn't."

The principal glared me silent. "Just yesterday she threatened one of the other girls in the school. There were witnesses."

Officer Oakes, who'd been listening and watching, now asked, "Is that what happened, Meg?"

Ignoring the policewoman, Dad faced MacMasters.

"My daughter says that the knife isn't hers. It must've been planted."

"Unlikely. I'm sorry to say that Meg has been a trouble-maker from day one." MacMasters folded his arms across his chest, rocked back on his heels. "There have been other incidents, too, Mr. Fairling. I have to consider the safety of the students at this school."

"*What* incidents?" Eyes narrowing, Dad took a step closer to the principal. Though he was at least six inches shorter than the principal, at that moment Dad looked as tough as MacMasters. "I want to know what you're talking about, and I want to know now."

The silence that followed my father's demand was loaded with so much tension that the office air seemed to crack with static electricity. Then a cool new voice asked, "Has the knife been dusted for prints?"

Ms. Llord was standing in the half-open doorway. "This is a closed meeting, Ms. Llord," MacMasters rumbled.

"I beg your pardon—the door was open, and I couldn't help overhearing. I merely point out that in a case of such gravity, the knife should definitely be checked for fingerprints."

Ms. Llord looked questioningly at Officer Oakes, who said, "It's not a police matter, Ms. Llord. No crime has been committed."

"The *prevention* of crime is the goal of law enforcement, Regina," the little lady came right back, and the policewoman winced even while she grinned.

"Yes, ma'am," she said. Then, taking a plastic bag, she slid it over the knife and removed it from my book bag. "Meg, you'll have to come downtown. We need your

158

fingerprints to see if they match the ones on this knife, okay?"

As I nodded numbly Mr. MacMasters had the last word. "This is a school matter. Meg, you are in clear violation of Massachusetts Laws Chapter 71, Section 37H. As such, I have no choice but to suspend you from South Regional High School. The suspension takes effect immediately."

Suspended.

The word seemed to come from a foreign language. Feeling numb and stupid, I just sat there and listened to Dad arguing with MacMasters.

The principal refused to give an inch. "The policy of the school is clearly stated on page forty-five of the student handbook. That handbook was handed out to all students at the beginning of the school year," he said. "Meg will be notified of a hearing, at which time you may present evidence and witnesses that will testify to her innocence." He paused and added that I was entitled to have representation at my hearing.

"You're damned straight she'll have representation," Dad retorted.

He was ripping as we finally left the principal's office to follow Officer Oakes down to the police station. Then, as we were getting into our car, he suddenly went, "Did you bring that knife to school, Meg?"

Tears clogged my throat, making it hard to speak. "I told you. I left my book bag in homeroom. *They* planted the knife between homeroom and when I picked it up at the office."

"*They*. What are you talking about?"

The tension of the morning knotted up in my stomach,

hurtling my by-now digested breakfast to my lips. I got out of the car, quick, and threw up on the ground.

Dad came around and rubbed my back like he used to do when I was sick as a little kid. "Don't try to be brave—just lie down in the back and close your eyes," he went. Then he added, "Meg, who did this to you?"

The change in his voice caught me by surprise. I'd been gearing myself up for Dad's anger, for more questioning, for suspicion and disbelief. Now something tight in my heart let go so suddenly that I began to bawl. Dad put his arms around me, and I leaned into his hug and heard him say, "I know you're telling the truth, Meg. I believe you."

He sounded like the old Dad, like my father before the store and Mimi and all our troubles. "It's all part of the game the Hunters are playing," I managed to say. "They're out to get me."

And then I told him everything. Told him without interruption until I came to the part about my visit to Mrs. Alvarez. "She warned me that I might be the Hunters' next victim," I told Dad. "I didn't believe her."

Did *Dad* believe me? I saw him frowning as he switched on the ignition and started our car. Suddenly he smacked the steering wheel. "I'd like to get my hands on Mr. Julius Angeli," he gritted. "The way he told it, *you* were the bad one. Meg, you should tell the police what you're telling me. Should've told them long ago."

I said that I couldn't. I had no proof. "I tried to tell Mr. MacMasters, but he wouldn't hear it."

Under his breath Dad muttered what he thought of MacMasters. As we rode down to police headquarters I continued to tell him what had been happening. When I got to the part about the index cards they'd circulated around school, Dad interrupted again. "They did *that*? And you didn't tell me about it?"

He insisted that I tell Officer Oakes the story. She listened carefully, even made notes. "What you're saying sounds similar to what Mrs. Alvarez told Officer Denton and me when her daughter committed suicide," she then went. "Say for a moment that I believe something's going on. It still comes down to one thing."

"Proof." I sighed.

"You got it. Right now it's their word against yours, Meg."

Officer Oakes said that all we could do was wait until the people at the lab dusted the knife for fingerprints, so Dad drove me back to the store, where I told my story again, to Mom. "I knew that kids teased each other, but this is incredible," she exclaimed when I'd finished. "I'd like to get my hands on those girls."

Then she, too, hugged me. How long had it been since both my parents had hugged me and told me they believed in what I said? "Too long," Mom said, as if she'd heard my unspoken thoughts. "You've held this awful secret too long, Meg. I blame myself. I was always too busy for you."

My heart did a funny little jump thing, but the brief moment of relief and happiness flickered out before it could take hold. "Diana's done it again," I mumbled. "She's beaten me *again*."

"I'm calling Arthur." Dad was all sharp and tense and businesslike as he snatched up the phone. "He'll know what to do."

Arthur Harrad was the folks' lawyer, who had known me since I was six. Mom looked more hopeful then, saying that if anybody could sort out this mess, Arthur could. "Meanwhile . . ."

She hesitated, not knowing what to say. Go home and do homework, Meg? Go running? Neither of them would do any good now that I was suspended from school and thus automatically thrown out of the South Regional Girls Cross-Country Team.

Before the full misery of that thought could engulf me, Dad said, "We could always use a hand around the store."

So I stayed and stacked boxes, made change, and answered the phone along with my folks. For the first time since it'd opened, I was truly grateful for Naturfoods. Working there not only gave me something to do but made me feel that I was a part of the team.

Later that afternoon, while I was sweeping out in the back, Jed came around with a stack of books sent courtesy of Ms. Llord.

Remembering Rea's face when she'd met me at the door of her house, I had this second of really unpleasant déjà vu. Victims, the both of us, except that I wasn't beaten yet. No way. And I sure wasn't about to hang myself because of the Hunters.

"Everybody's talking about the knife at school," Jed was saying. Then, in one of his typical subject shifts, he went, "I'm sorry for getting on your case yesterday."

"No, you were right," I told him. "I'm the one who's sorry. I set myself up for this. I just didn't think they'd go this far."

His ears got red. "It's not you who should be sorry, it's them. They think they're so big and wonderful, but they're just a sorry bunch of sickos." Jed paused for

162

breath. "But the Hunters are out of their league this time. They don't know who they're messing with."

I said sure, we were a couple of superheroes. "I don't mean us, you goofus," Jed scoffed. "In class today Ms. Llord gave us a lecture about people being innocent until proven guilty."

I told Jed how, in MacMasters's office, Lord Doom had stood up for me, too, and insisted that the knife be fingerprinted. "But even Ms. Llord can't keep me on the track team." I sighed.

Thinking of how hard I'd worked for Prudhomme, thinking of everything that had happened to me that day, I cried myself to sleep. But next morning brought better news. Mr. Harrad, our lawyer, called to say he was going to request that my hearing before the principal be held as soon as possible.

"I checked with the police, and Meg's fingerprints were *not* found on that knife," he said. "I'd say that's a darn good indication that she didn't bring the knife to school."

The hearing with Mr. MacMasters was called for that afternoon, after school. Dad closed the store and all of us met Mr. Harrad at South Regional. When we got there, kids were pouring out of the doors and onto waiting buses. Mom nudged me.

"There's Karen," she exclaimed.

Munch was walking ten yards away. She was with Kenny, Diana, and Vi, and behind her Cass and B.K. walked hand in hand. None of them looked our way. "Which one is Diana?" Mom asked. "I'm going to talk to her and tell her—"

"Hold on, Nolly," Mr. Harrad warned. "A confrontation

163

like that isn't going to help. Let's get into that meeting and see what we can do to get Meg back into school."

We were early, so we had to wait while Mr. MacMasters finished talking to some people in his office. While we were waiting, Ms. Llord joined us. "I requested permission to attend the meeting," she explained. "Unless you or your parents object, Meg?"

I was introducing her to my folks when Mr. MacMasters came out of his office. "You requested this hearing be pushed up, Mr. Fairling," he said as if to say, Let's get it over with.

In a stiff voice, Dad introduced Mom and Mr. Harrad. With equal coldness, the principal acknowledged them.

Mr. Harrad said, "Meg is being suspended because she brought a knife to school, yet this police report proves that *no* prints were found on the knife."

He laid an official-looking report on the desk. "She might have been wearing gloves," Mr. MacMasters came back.

"I wasn't—" I began, but Ms. Llord cut me off.

"It would seem strange to me," she said in her driest voice, "that anybody who intended to stab a classmate would purposely go to the trouble of wiping off the blade and the handle of her weapon *before* the attack. What would be the point? It is completely illogical. I can understand someone wiping the weapon after the deed," she added, "but not before."

"Someone obviously put the knife into Meg's book bag," Mr. Harrad agreed. "This incident is in keeping with the harassment Meg has been subjected to of late."

"According to my daughter, she attempted to tell you about this harassment, but you wouldn't give her the time

164

of day." My dad broke in. "It seems to me that you've been listening to only one side of the story."

For the first time since I'd known him, Mr. MacMasters looked uncertain. "All right, Meg," he allowed, "what *has* been going on?"

I started with what had happened to Rea and then went right down the line with what the Hunters had done to me. By the time I'd finished, the room was really silent.

"You have only to telephone Mrs. Jameson, principal of the Chisolm Middle School, to confirm what Meg has said," our attorney suggested. "Mrs. Jameson told me that in February of this year Mrs. George Alvarez complained that Diana Angeli, Violet Rochard, and Cassandra Johns were harassing her late daughter, Rea. The matter was dropped because there was no evidence to prove her allegations. However, there is a definite correlation between the kind of harassment that Mrs. Alvarez detailed and what has been happening to Meg. Obscene notes sent to teachers. So-called advertisements touting the 'party girl' line, and so on—here is a list."

Mr. Harrad plunked another paper down on Mr. MacMasters's desk. "I will most certainly investigate this matter," the principal promised. He paused a beat and then added stiffly, "In light of what I've just learned, Meg's suspension is lifted. I'm sorry, Meg, that you were put through such an ordeal. I fully intend to get to the bottom of it."

Mom and I hugged each other. Dad somewhat grudgingly shook our principal's hand. He also fervently thanked Ms. Llord for her support.

Ms. Llord accepted the thanks as if it were her due. Then she turned to me. I thought she was about to congratulate me, but the smile on my face congealed as she announced, "Tomorrow there will be a test on Chapter Six: Eukarotic Cells. If you have completed yesterday's assignment, you have nothing to worry about."

TEN

IT WAS LIKE one of those good-news, bad-news stories: hey, Meg, the good news is that you get to come back to school and can be part of the cross-country team again. The bad news is that you've got a test waiting for you in Lord Doom's class.

Jed promised he'd review eukarotic cells during an after-practice run along Spruce Way. So, picture this. Here we are running. Jed is for once running slow, and gestures with both hands as he explains about animal and plant cells and their parts: nucleus, cytoplasm, cell membrane, and mitochondria—

"Hold on!" I yelled, because one of my shoelaces had become untied.

Deep into the way cell membranes regulated cell-to-cell interactions, Jed didn't even hear me. "Hey," I yelled, "wait up, willya?"

At this he glanced over his shoulder, stumbled, and fell. *Boom!* That was how quick it was. Then he yelled in pain.

I started to run over to him, saw just in time what looked to be a hollow in the road, jumped over it, and fell on my knees next to Jed.

"Are you okay?" I yelped.

He tried to sit up, went, "Aah, *damn* it, my knee. It's all crapped up."

Scared, not knowing what to do, I stared from Jed's already swelling right knee to his pain-drawn face. "What *happened*?" I babbled. "Is it broken?"

"Sprained, I think. Must've stepped into a hole," he groaned.

Looking over my shoulder, I noted that Jed hadn't seen the hole because it had been covered over with autumn leaves. I got shakily to my feet, kicked at the leaves at the edge of the hole, and saw that it was really a trench that extended from one side of the dirt road to the other. The earth had been newly turned.

Somebody had dug this ditch recently and camouflaged it with leaves. "They knew we ran here," I stammered. "They were banking that I'd stumble into this and—Jed, I'm so sorry. It was me they wanted to get."

"Well, they did just fine, huh? No way am I going to run anywhere with this knee." Suddenly Jed slammed both fists onto the ground. "*Damn* them," he yelled.

His voice cracked. Drawing his good knee into his chest, Jed dropped his face down onto it. His shoulders shook. All the months of running and training—and now in one second the chance to compete in the state meet had been snatched away from him. And it was because the Hunters hated me. Because Jed was my friend.

"I'm sorry," I repeated, and because words couldn't begin to tell him how rotten-bad I felt, I got back on my knees beside him and put my arms around him and cried, too. After a long minute he sighed.

"It's okay," he said, his voice husky with his own tears.

"No, it's not!"

168

"None of this is your fault." He put his arms around me, too, and with his damp, hard-boned cheek pressed against mine, ordered, "Quit crying, okay? Quit being such a goofus, Goofus."

"I should've known they'd pull something like this. Should have *known*. Jed, I'm going to get Diana Angeli if it's the last thing I do."

"How?" Jed asked practically.

I had no answer to that, but here in Jed's arms, with his breath against my ear and his sweat-damp hair tickling my cheek, I knew I was going to do it. Somehow. Some-*way*. The Hunters had hurt two of my friends, hurt them bad. "Never again," I vowed. "I won't let them."

Jed shifted his hurt knee, yelped in pain, and let go of me to massage it. "Just how are we going to get the Hunters?" he repeated.

Hunkering back on my heels, I wiped my eyes on the back of my hand and scowled at the deadly fissure in the road. "MacMasters is watching them, but that's not enough. We need help from someone who really hates the Hunters. Like Mrs. Alvarez, maybe."

Jed pointed out that Mrs. Alvarez hadn't even been able to help her own daughter. Then he instructed me to run to the nearest pay phone and call his mom. "Tell Ma to bring a shovel," he added. "We've got to fill in this ditch before somebody else gets hurt."

I was about to start off when he added, "Meg, something's really funny about this."

I said, sure, it was hilarious. "I mean," Jed said patiently, "that this isn't the Hunters' usual MO. They like to be sneaky, pull surprises when you're not expecting them. This ditch is mean, ugly, and as obvious as the nose on my face."

"You mean, Kenny or B.K.—"

"I'll bet you anything that Diana never told those scuzzbags to go dig a hole," Jed fumed. "I'll bet anything they did this on their own. I'd like to get them, boy. *Man,* I would like to get them for this."

But we'd never get any of them without—you guessed it—proof. I chewed over that thought while we waited for Mrs. Berringer and later, after she'd driven me home, I didn't give myself time to chicken out. I looked up the Alvarezes' number in the phone book and made the call.

The dial tone whirred and clicked a few times before a little girl answered and said that Mamacita was sleeping. Then I heard Mrs. Alvarez talking in the background, and then her sleepy voice came on the phone asking who was calling. When I told her, she said yes, she remembered me, and what news did I have?

There was only one kind of news Mrs. Alvarez wanted to hear, so I told her that Diana and the others could finally be headed for trouble. "But they're still doing awful things," I added. "They got me suspended from school for a couple of days, and today, they hurt a friend of mine. I'd like to get them, but—"

"*But* there is no proof of what they do," Mrs. Alvarez said heavily. "I know it. It was the same with me."

But she perked up when I told her about Mr. Harrad, our attorney, talking to the principal at the Chisolm Middle School. "You mean that finally Mrs. Jameson believes that Rea never did those bad things at the school?"

Her voice had suddenly come alive, and I felt my own hopes rise. *Maybe.* "If you could write down a list of everything that those girls did to Rea," I suggested, "it might help. We could give the list to Mr. Harrad or to Mr. MacMasters."

170

"It hurts to remember that time—" Mrs. Alvarez checked herself. "But I will try. Perhaps, as you say, it will help. And I will pray for you, Meg."

I thanked her for her good thoughts, but all the prayers in the world couldn't help me next day when I faced Ms. Llord's nerve-paralyzing test. Even Jed, who was in a soft cast and crutches, having definitely sprained his knee, allowed that he'd had some trouble with the test while I was so disasterized that I could hardly remember my own name.

At any other time I'd have worried about failing the test, but too much was going on for me to be scared of Ms. Llord. I was sure that Diana would fight back. As Mimi might say, I was waiting for the other shoe to drop.

Nothing happened. A week went by. Still nothing; except that Ms. Llord began a lab showing us about DNA, mRNA, tRNA and amino acids in the role of protein synthesis; except that Diana was elected our freshman rep to the student council.

Two weeks, and I was one of the five girls Prudhomme sent to the league meet, where I clocked in at nineteen minutes twenty-five—good enough to make it to the A-Class meet.

If Prudhomme'd been hard to live with before, he was now a maniac. "Remember, once you step on the line, you have no friends," he drilled. "Thinking about other runners will slow yourself down. Focus, and you can make Springfield happen!"

My folks came to cheer me on at the A-Class meet. Mimi made me wear her lucky ring, the one she'd worn when she'd climbed the Matterhorn. Jed limped beside me and the other runners as we walked to the starting line.

171

"You can do it," he kept repeating. "You've done it before, Meg, right? Be strong, okay? It's a cakewalk, just three miles. . . ."

But I didn't do it. Maybe it was the unfamiliar terrain, or a mega-case of nerves that shook me as I waited on that line for the starting gun, but though I ran myself half-blind, my time put me at 19:42, seconds out of the running. My only consolation was that two guys from the SR Boys' Cross-Country Team did manage to qualify for the Springfield meet.

And still, there was nothing from the Hunters. By now we were into November, and Jed's knee was doing so much better that he was walking without crutches or a cane.

"I have to exercise it," he explained to Mimi when he dropped by unexpectedly during one Sunday visit. "See?" He waggled his knee experimentally and winced a little. "The doctor doesn't understand how come I didn't rip every single tendon when I fell."

"The rewards of a good constitution," Mimi said. "Are you feeding the constitution enough, Jed? You look skinnier than when I saw you last."

Seeing Jed walk through the door, Mom had set another place at the table. He swore that he'd just eaten supper but allowed as he'd try the pot roast, anyway. "This is great," he said, chomping heartily. "We had ham and scalloped potatoes at home."

Mimi opened her mouth, but before she could start in on the cooking at Meadowriver, Dad said, "I spoke to MacMasters on Friday, Mother, about those girls who've been harassing Meg. He says that he's been investigating, but so far, nothing."

Dad scowled at his plate. Mom put a hand on his arm

172

and said, "It's bound to come out in the end, Jerry. In the meantime at least they're leaving Meg alone."

She served Jed a huge piece of apple pie, and he scarfed it up as if he'd never seen pie before. I looked at him in awe, wondering how anybody so thin could eat so much and *stay* thin.

"It's not fair." I sighed.

Dad misunderstood. "It sure isn't, but MacMasters says his hands are tied unless he has proof positive."

"I don't think those girls will hurt someone else," Mom said. "The fact that someone finally had the gumption to stand up to them has taught them a lesson."

I saw Jed open his mouth and then close it. He looked thoughtful all during the rest of the visit, and when Dad offered to drive him home on the way to taking Mimi back, he agreed as though his mind was miles away.

While Mom was packing pie for Mimi to take to Silky Sulieman, I walked Jed into the backyard. "What were you going to say back there?" I asked.

Jed didn't answer right away. It was a peaceful autumn night with a full moon and loads of insects doing their end-of-autumn thing in Mimi's chrysanthemum bed. Finally, he said, "Are you going to Springfield this weekend?" I said I'd be traveling up with Prudhomme and our team on Saturday morning. "We have a cousin who lives in Pittsfield, so I'm leaving Friday afternoon with the folks and staying there a couple of days. I'll see you at the meet."

"You should've been running in that meet." I sighed.

"I may not have made it past the league meet, anyway." Then Jed added, "The Hunters haven't quit, y'know. They may be finished with *you,* but they're not down for the count."

173

A cold chill that had nothing to do with the crisp autumn weather ruffled the hairs on the base of my neck. I'd had that feeling, too.

"I think that they're just waiting for the heat to die down," Jed went on. "Then they'll start again."

Knowing he was right, I argued that they'd have to know MacMasters was after them. "Normal people would worry about that," Jed agreed, "but I think Diana's sure she's smarter than anyone else. She *is* smart. Look at the way she got elected to the student council even with MacMasters watching her. She's got to take that as a sign that she can get away with anything."

The beautiful night was suddenly full of menace. "I could be wrong," Jed went on. "Maybe they won't be able to hold it together like they used to in middle school. SR is the big leagues, and the Hunters may find they can't push everybody's buttons like they used to. Maybe, finally, they'll stop."

He spoke so confidently that for no reason I felt a lump form under my breastbone. "I couldn't have gotten this far without you," I told him. He told me to put a sock in it. "Shut up, I'm trying to be serious," I said. "When this all started, I was going through the worst time. New school, and Mimi having to go to Meadowriver, and Karen finding new best friends."

The insects stopped shrieking and rasping, and in the sudden silence my voice sounded too loud. I lowered it to add rather lamely, "Thanks for being there, okay?"

Jed didn't say anything like, what are friends for, or no problem, or don't be a goofus. Instead, he put both arms around me and held me.

We hugged each other the way we'd done the day he hurt his knee—but then we'd been trying to console each other. *This* closeness reminded me more of the seconds before the big fireworks on the Fourth when you're holding your breath waiting for the skies to turn to fire. Or of the millisecond between the time you jump off the diving board and hit the cool water waiting underneath.

Waiting, with the prickle of goose bumps marching across my arms, I held my breath. Held it waiting for Jed to kiss me.

"Next year we'll both be running in Springfield," he told me.

But right then cross-country didn't seem important. "We'll deal with the Hunters." I nodded, afraid to speak and break the magic of the moment. "We'll stop them, Meg," Jed went.

And bent and kissed me, sealing that promise.

On Monday Ms. Llord announced our grades to date. Jed got an A. For me, there was a C-.

"Ordinarily," she informed me, "I would let that grade stand. But because your life has been somewhat turbulent these past few weeks, Meg, I will give you a chance to raise your grade."

What sounded like a great favor was actually torture. It meant that I had to study like a mad person and then stay after school on Friday to take what Lord Doom called a "comprehensive test" seventh period. Jed sympathized, but his mind was more on Springfield than on my misery.

"Anyway," he went, "when I see you up at Springfield, you can tell me whether you survived or not."

With my butt on the line, I pulled an all-nighter and, on Friday after school, sat glazed-eyed and clenched-jawed at my desk and wrote and wrote and wrote while

175

other, more fortunate kids whooped in the halls or headed home on the bus. By the time I'd finished my test, my wrist had cramped and my brain matched the wrist. I didn't need Lord Doom to ask if I'd done my best.

I muttered an answer, and she clicked her tongue. "Don't mumble," she reproved. "Either say what you have to say or say nothing."

I took a deep breath and to my horror heard myself say clearly, "My goose is pissed."

The second the words were out of my mouth, I felt all the blood drain down from my head to my legs, leaving me icy cold. I stared at Ms. Llord in absolute horror, and for a second she stared back at me.

"Go on," she then said. "Get out of here."

As fast as my numbed legs could carry me, I staggered out. As I left the room I heard something that made my head spin. Ms. Llord was laughing!

There she was whooping and hollering in that classroom, and I realized what I'd never have guessed back in September. Ms. Llord wasn't an ice-blooded, incredibly smart lady who could terrorize even Mr. MacMasters with the flash of an eye. She was a *human*, and a good person, and she had a sense of humor. With those unbelievable revelations whirring about my brain, I stumbled toward my locker in the two-hundred wing. As I passed the corner that led to the locker, I heard a giggle and a familiar voice say, "Cass, for Pete's sake, hurry up!"

It was Karen's voice, breathless with excitement, a little scared. As the thought sank in, I heard Cass's familiar, chirpy voice reply calmly, "Don't get your gym shorts into a knot, I've got it. Now all we do is slide this baby in—"

Looking around at the row of lockers, I saw Karen and

Cass. Karen had her back to me as if shielding Cass, who was pushing something inside one of the lockers.

"What are you doing?" I demanded.

They both looked around, quick. Cass grabbed for whatever it was she was pushing into the locker, but years of running track have given me good reflexes. I slid between her and the open locker.

"Get out of the way," Cass twittered. Karen stammered, "What are you doing here, Meg? We were just getting something from Cass's locker—"

"This isn't Cass's locker. It's Doris Leo's. Is she your new victim?"

Karen looked a little sick, but Cass tossed her head and chirped, "If you *must* know, Doris asked us to put something into her locker for her."

"Sure she did," I came right back. "Like you're friendly with 'the freshman-class dork,' I think you called her?" Cass bit her lip. "What did she do, get a better grade than you, or what?"

I reached in my book bag, took a tissue, and carefully, so as not to get my own fingerprints on it, snagged the thing that Cass had been sliding into Doris's locker. It was a small plastic bag full of something that looked like dried leaves.

"I guess that's how you put drugs in Rea's locker, huh?"

I wanted to yell the accusation at Cass, but my voice was shaking because I was so mad. Right there and then I could have torn her apart. "Give me that!" Cass yipped.

She tried to snatch the plastic bag from me. I shoved her, and she went staggering back against Karen. "Leave me alone," she piped, "or—"

177

"Or you'll call for help?" I demanded savagely. "Go ahead. Let's see if MacMasters will come running."

"Megs," Karen said in a low voice, "please don't do this."

Furiously, I rounded on her. "You wrote that snappy little bit for the paper about Mimi, didn't you?"

Karen's plump cheeks drained of color, and she bit her lip. Sick of looking at them, I pulled out a handful of tissues, which I wrapped carefully around the little plastic bag. I then settled it gently into the book bag.

"You can't prove a thing," Cass blustered.

A girl from my track team chanced to walk by the lockers. She looked at us curiously before going on her way. "Hey, Helen," I called after her. "Tell Mr. Mac—"

I didn't get any further, for Karen yanked me back. "Megs," she wailed, "Megs, *please* don't say anything." Tears were welling into Karen's eyes and sliding down her round cheeks. "If Moms finds out, she'll—Megs, I swear, I'll never do this again."

Cass said nothing, but she was looking less sure of herself now. "We'll leave Doris alone," Karen went on. "Really, we will. Megs, we've been friends for years—"

I started to walk away, but she ran after me. "Megs," she pleaded, "don't tell MacMasters. Okay, I was wrong, I admit it. But Diana's so cool, and I never realized what they were doing—I thought they were such fat—I mean, such really cool girls—"

She swabbed at her tears with fingers that had been gnawed almost raw. I wanted to tell Munch that I was going to report everything to MacMasters right away, but when I remembered Mrs. Tierney's mean eyes, the words stuck in my throat.

So I just left Karen standing there and walked toward

178

the office, remembering bits and pieces of what had been the most important friendship of my life. A jigsaw puzzle of whispered secrets. The time Gorki'd been sideswiped by a car and Karen'd helped me carry her home. The day Munch's mother freaked because she'd sneaked out to the movies, and hit her, and Karen'd come running to our house—

Past, all past and gone, I told myself, and walked into the office, passed the secretary who was talking on the phone, and knocked on MacMasters's office door.

It was empty. He wasn't there. I felt both disappointed and relieved when the secretary told me he'd gone to a meeting with the superintendent, because that meant I didn't have to make a decision right away.

So I rode the late bus home knowing what I should do, what my folks would tell me to do. I knew what Jed would do in my shoes, what I ought to do, but Munch's scared face and her poor, bitten fingers and hands haunted me. "Leave me alone," I told that bothersome memory. "You played the game, you've got to pay the price. Dance with the devil, and you'll get burned—"

I broke off on one of Mimi's favorite quotes and knew who I needed to talk to. Back at the house I just took time to toss my book bag inside the door and then headed into the back to get my bike. I was wheeling it out of the tool-shed when a girl on a racing bicycle swooped up to the front of the house. It took a second before I realized it was Diana.

"Meg," she called, "we need to talk."

"No, we don't," I shouted back. "I'm going to tell MacMasters what I saw—period."

"I'm not here to try and intimidate you. You're too smart and too strong for that." She stood straddling her

179

expensive bike, her strawberry-blond hair rippling in the wind, her face flushed and earnest. "First, I want to tell you I'm sorry for those things we did to you. I should've known you'd be too strong to break."

There was this small, stupid corner inside my head that was pleased even now by the respect in her voice. Diana, I reminded myself, was smart enough to twist people into doing what she wanted.

"Save it—it isn't going to work," I told her. "Cass's fingerprints are on that plastic bag, and besides, Helen Tarner was walking by. She saw them, too."

"She saw nothing," Diana came right back. "It'll be your word against Cass's and Karen's, Meg. I'm not worried, not really. I'm here talking to you because I respect you."

She leaned forward over the handlebars, her green eyes narrowed against the sun. "Look, if you accuse us, you'll have a hard time proving we did *anything* wrong. On the other hand, if you don't say anything, I'll make it up to you."

I started to wheel my bike toward the front of the house, and Diana followed me. "I'll tell you who dug that ditch in the woods, the one your boyfriend stumbled into and hurt his knee."

I whirled to face her. Like the queen of cool she fronted me, her green gaze holding mine as if she was the one in charge, not me. "Go on," I said.

"As you've probably guessed, Kenny dug that ditch." Diana's tone turned mocking. "He's so dumb, he thought that nobody would suspect he did it. When he told me about it, I could've hit the big jerk."

"But you didn't. You just smiled at him and told him

how great he was," I cut in. "He's useful to you still, isn't he, Diana?"

Ignoring this, she went on, "I'll give you proof that Kenny dug that ditch. You can report him to the police and get him into big trouble. He *deserves* to be in trouble for what he did to Jed."

She actually sounded indignant. She was offering me Kenny in exchange for Cass and Karen. "What proof are we talking about?" She just smiled. "I guess then you and Kenny broke up," I added.

"Break up with *Kenny*?" She looked at me with contempt. "He may have thought we were going out, but *I* never did. He's boring."

"But useful, and he has cool wheels and a driver's license." Diana shrugged. "I guess you're stringing him along till something better comes along."

Another shrug. "That ditch was all his idea, you know, just like chasing you in the woods was that brainless B.K.'s." She tossed back her gleaming hair. "Nothing like that will ever happen again, Meg. I promise."

Rea's despairing face flickered through my mind and was replaced by Doris Leo. Doris with her sinus snuffle would be the perfect victim because nobody would care if she got picked on and a lot of people would even think it was funny. "No," I told Diana. "Nothing like that is ever going to happen again."

Just then, the phone began to ring inside the house. Leaving my bike where it was, I started up the stairs. As quick as a flash, Diana dismounted and ran up the stairs after me. "Think what it'll do to Karen," she urged.

"Did Karen take an oath to your moon goddess, too?"

Till that second I guess I had some doubts about Wes Peterson's bizarre accusations. Now, as I watched Diana's face change, grow harder, sharper, I knew he'd told me the truth.

She leaned across and, putting her hand flat against the door, held it shut. "You'd better watch your step," she hissed. "If you talk, Meg, you'd better keep an eye on your shadow, 'cause from now on we'll be right behind you."

Wordless, I pushed her hand away and opened the door. "You think you've got us, but you don't," Diana went on. "Cass and Karen won't say a word. Nobody else will, either. And there's no real proof to link me to that bag of grass. You're the one who'll be in *big* trouble."

"Go to hell, Diana."

I went into the house, slammed the door shut, then stood with my back against the closed door as if that could keep her out. My heart was thumping like crazy, and I was shaking, and I hated myself for being so weak. "I'm not the one in trouble," I muttered. "It's you, Diana."

All I needed to do was call the store and tell Dad what I'd found and let him phone MacMasters. That was all I had to do, and yet I still did nothing. I hated Diana and the others and wouldn't have cared if they were thrown into jail. But—Karen?

The first time Mimi had taken off on us, Munch had helped me search for her. We'd found her and brought her back before my folks got home, and Karen hadn't told anyone about that, ever. She'd been my good friend then, and yet now I was going to rat on her.

"It's not the same thing," I muttered, but I still couldn't bear to make that phone call.

But I had to do it. Had to. Slowly, I went to the phone in the kitchen, saw that the message taker was blinking, and snapped it on. Steeling myself to hear Karen's frantic pleading, I heard instead an adult voice distorted by the bad tape.

"Mrs. Fairling?" it said, "this is Laura Jordans, director of Meadowriver. The Naturfoods store number keeps ringing busy, so I'm trying you at home. I'm sorry to tell you this, but Mrs. Castleway is missing."

ELEVEN

IT HAD TO be some kind of mistake—had to! I punched the Repeat button, and the message repeated word for word. Mimi'd taken off again.

Insides bunching with familiar fear, I called Meadowriver right away. The agitated staff member who took my call told me Mimi still hadn't been found. I next tried the store, and the line rang busy. They had call waiting at Naturfoods, so either my parents were talking to two people on the line, or something was wrong with the phone.

Not knowing what else to do, I grabbed my bike and took off along Mountain Road. Had Mimi seemed somehow different lately? Sunday was the last time I'd seen her, on account of my having to study for Lord Doom's test, but I'd talked to her every night. Last night I'd caught her just before she went to dinner, and she was in a good mood because Silky was waiting to "escort" her into dinner.

Then why—*how*? I tried those questions on Ruth Winton, the first person I ran into when I got to Meadowriver. "We're not sure," the first-floor nurse supervisor replied distractedly. Then she told me that the director'd reached my parents and that they were on their way.

184

Just then, a familiar voice boomed my name, and I saw Ms. Vera Pors waving to me from a chair in the lobby. Next to her little Miss Harriway looked smaller and grayer than ever.

"Isn't it awful what's happened?" Ms. Pors bellowed as I hurried over to her. "I never would have believed Silky would be taken like that."

She went on to inform me that Silky Sulieman'd had a massive heart attack yesterday evening. "We were having dinner, and then suddenly he turned all red and fell down on the floor." Ms. Pors raised one hamlike hand and smacked it against her thigh. "*Whomp!* Just like that. It gave me a turn, I can tell you, lamb. Nearly passed out myself."

She paused, allowing Miss Harriway to add, "Your grandma was seated right next to him. Right next to him. She was on the floor beside him in a minute, tried to massage his chest and all." She shook her delicate white head. "Stayed right with him till the ambulance came to take him to Chisolm Hospital."

Suddenly everything made sense. "She's gone to find Silky," I exclaimed.

That simple, logical explanation filled me with incredible relief. Mimi hadn't taken off in a confused daze; she'd had a purpose in mind. Chisolm Hospital was on the other end of town, and Mimi knew basically where it was. Since she'd stayed with Silky until the paramedics came, she might even have gotten directions.

I left the old ladies talking to each other, headed for my bike, and pedaled off in the general direction of Chisolm Hospital. I'd gone a few miles before it hit me that the hospital would be the first place the police would look. If they hadn't reported Mimi found by now, it meant that she wasn't there.

But not necessarily, I argued with myself. Maybe Mimi had gotten lost on one of the side streets. There were so *many* streets that it was really easy to lose your bearings.

Okay, so I'd search the side streets. It had clouded over, and against the leaden gray the trees looked almost startling in their autumn colors. Huge golden leaves drifted past me as I pedaled up and down streets and avenues until I found myself on a wider road that led toward the sound of busy traffic. A sign told me that I was approaching well-traveled Route 27—

My thoughts broke off. Traffic on the busy highway had slowed down for a moment, slowed enough for me to see someone sitting on the median island.

"Mimi?"

The old lady with white hair was dressed in a neat lavender sweater and matching slacks and wore fluffy blue bedroom slippers on her feet. She was sitting on the grassy island, her legs drawn up into her chest. She was leaning forward, and at first I thought she was being sick.

Then I saw her hands. Fingers bent and moving rapidly, Mimi was playing a piano that only she could see. Her body swayed from side to side, and her closed eyes and the satisfied smile on her lips told me that what she played was beautiful to her.

I got off my bike, dropped it on the sidewalk, and waded through traffic to her little island. Just as she ignored the noise of the traffic, she didn't seem to hear me call her name.

Oblivious to me, her fingers stroked the air, and as those strong, delicate fingers played notes that only she could hear, her smile grew even more tender. I put my hand on her shoulder. "Mimi," I pleaded, "c'mon, Mimi."

Instead of responding, she began to whistle, and I recognized the lullaby with which she'd sung me to sleep. Plopping down on my knees beside her, I tried to coax her to move, but she didn't even know I was there.

People were staring at us from their car windows, gawking, pointing. I glared at the rubberneckers, hating them. I felt sick and embarrassed by their curiosity, and my chest was so sore I could hardly breathe. Not so much because I was sorry for Mimi but because I didn't know what to do. Because what I *wanted* to do most right then was to get away from this wild-eyed, white-haired stranger who had once been my grandmother.

"Mimi, come *on*—"

Suddenly she turned to look at me, and I thought I saw something flicker in her eyes. Confusion, recognition, sorrow? It was gone before I could place it. Then Mimi said, "Truth."

Her voice was forced and thick. "Truth," she repeated firmly. Then she added, "No more time."

Then she returned to playing her invisible instrument. I hugged my knees to my hurting chest, knowing that even though she had no idea what she'd just said, my grandmother was making terrible sense.

Mimi had run out of time. She wasn't going to get well. She would never leave Meadowriver to come home to her room and her own bed. I couldn't ever come to her for advice or understanding because the Mimi I knew had changed and would continue to change. Pitilessly, her sickness would grind her down, until there was nothing left of the person she'd once been.

That was one truth. And there was another situation, one that had nothing to do with Mimi. I had to make a decision on the Hunters before time ran out for Munch.

Diana could promise me anything she wanted, but she wouldn't change. The Hunters had enjoyed playing their vicious power games so long that it wouldn't be easy for them to quit. Maybe the high they got out of tormenting helpless victims was like taking a drug. Possibly they'd lie low for a while, but eventually they'd start again on someone else. They wouldn't be able to stay away from the twisted pleasure of it.

"They" meaning Diana, Cass, and Vi—but Munch hadn't been one of the Hunters for a long time. Maybe *she* could change, if I had the guts to act right away.

There was a whir of sound, a flash of lights, and a police cruiser drew up to the island where we were. It stopped, and I put an arm around Mimi's shoulders.

"It's time to go," I told her.

And as if she'd finally heard me, my grandmother stopped her restless playing and her whistling and, turning to face me, clapped her hands together in applause.

"Bravo," she told me earnestly. "Oh, bravo!"

Afterward, when Mimi had been settled back in Meadowriver, I told my folks about what I'd seen Karen and Cass do. Dad right away phoned the police, and we drove over to the Chisolm police station.

On the ride down, I felt sick to my stomach. My dad didn't have that problem. "All criminals get careless," he exulted. "Let's see them wriggle out of this one, right, Nolly?"

Mom agreed, but her eyes were full of pain and far away. I knew she was thinking of Mimi.

Mimi, sedated, quiet, and lying in her bed at Meadowriver—it was a relief to push that image aside and give my statement to Officer Oakes. I also handed over the Kleenex-wrapped plastic bag Cass had put in Doris Leo's locker, and Officer Oakes called in a Captain Harley, her boss.

Captain Harley confirmed that the bag had marijuana in it. He told us that he was going to send separate squad cars to pick up Karen and Cass. Their parents would be asked to follow.

"If, as Meg says, their fingerprints are on this bag," Captain Harley went on, "the girls will be charged with possession of drugs. Booking procedures will be initiated in the presence of their parents."

"What else?" Dad wanted to know. "They've done a lot of terrible things, and not just to my daughter, either. These girls hounded Rea Alvarez to death."

Officer Oakes said she was working on that angle, so I told her about my conversation with Mrs. Alvarez and how she was going to write down a list of all the things that the Hunters had done to Rea. Officer Oakes looked interested and said she'd call her right away.

Mr. MacMasters had also been informed of the incident. We waited at the precinct house till he got there, and I had to tell my story all over again. As I was doing so, two officers escorted Karen into the police station.

Mrs. Tierney was right behind them, and the way she glared at me caused my stomach to knot up. Munch kept her head down, but I saw her chewing on the back of her hand.

Mom had seen Mrs. Tierney giving me the evil eye. She asked if I had to stay any longer, and Officer Oakes said no, she'd be in touch if I was needed. "Then let's go home." Mom sighed.

She and Dad walked me toward the door. As we reached it a police cruiser drove up with Cass. Right on its tail came a sleek Mercedes with two adults—probably her parents. They didn't even look our way, but Cass cut me a vicious look as we passed her on the stairs.

"Watch it," she whispered. "*Watch* your back, Meg."

It was the last straw. In our car, going home, I started to think of Munch's misery, of Cass's hate, and mostly of Mimi, and that brought on the shakes.

"It's been an awful day"—Mom sighed—"and my head is splitting. I'm going home and getting into a hot bath. Then I'll make us some soup."

Dad said that he had some stuff to do back at the store. "But I'll be home in an hour at most," he promised. "Soup sounds good."

"She was doing so *well*." Mom sounded close to tears.

"Don't beat yourself up, Nolly." Dad reached across the seat and rubbed the back of Mom's neck. "She's strong. She'll get better again."

But would she? That question, never really put into words but clear in all our minds, hung heavy as Dad let Mom and me off at the house and drove away. "Mom?" I whispered.

"I don't know, Meg. I just don't *know*." My mother took a deep breath, gave my shoulder a wordless little pat, and then went into the house. Not wanting to follow right away, I leaned up against the door and watched the early stars shining pale through the twilight. Mimi had told me the names of the constellations, but I'd forgotten. Why had I forgotten so many things she'd taught me, when everything in the world reminded me of her?

Like the piano. I went into the house and there in the corner of the living room, looking dusty and old and tired, was the old upright. I opened the lid, touched the keys lightly so as not to make sound. *Glissando, legato, staccato*—they were just words, now. "Channel your emotion," she had told me so often. "Create beauty, not distortion." Now the whole world seemed distorted.

Gorki came and rubbed herself against my legs, demanding dinner. I went into the kitchen with her and was opening a can of whitefish when I saw the blink-flash of the message taker. I flipped on the machine, and Jed's voice, garbled because of the old tape, announced he was back in town.

Apparently, the Springfield meet had been called off because of some problem that I couldn't figure out on account of the horrible tape. Then Jed added, "We're over at Coach Hargen's right now. Maybe you could come over?"

Jed's coach lived just a couple of miles away, and that gave me a thought. *I* had news for Jed, too, and I could use a short run more than anything, clear the cobwebs, as Mimi might say.

I went upstairs, called through the bathroom door to tell Mom I was taking a quick run, and went to put on my reflectors. As I was hurrying through warm-ups I pictured Jed's face when I told him that I'd caught two of the Hunters. I rehearsed what I'd tell him about Diana's coming to see me. And then, finally, I'd have to tell him about Mimi.

What would I say? How could I put into words what I'd felt on that grassy island? Moving that miserable, shameful thought around in my mind, I turned onto Fern Way. I was wondering what could have happened to stop the meet, when I heard something rustle in the trees that bordered this part of Fern. I looked around, saw nothing. Probably a squirrel chasing a late harvest, I thought.

There was another rustle, louder than the first, and then suddenly a dark figure jumped out of the trees and rushed me. Instinctively I pivoted to run back the way I'd come and found Kenny blocking my path.

"Gotcha," he chortled.

My brain hadn't yet gotten it together enough to be scared. I remember shouting something like, "Get out of my way," as I charged Kenny.

He hunkered down as if to block me, but I feinted out of his clutching hands and was about to break the school record for the hundred-yard dash when somebody grabbed me from behind. One iron arm coiled around my waist, a hand twisted into my hair, yanking back. "One word out of you," B.K. snarled, "and you're dead meat."

There was liquor on his breath and enough viciousness in his voice to tell me he meant business. Kenny alone I might be able to outwit and outmaneuver, but B.K. was too strong. "You're gonna go back to the police station and tell them you didn't see Cass and Karen," B.K. snarled. "You're gonna tell them you made a mistake."

In the silence that followed B.K.'s words, I could hear Kenny wheezing and squeaking like a door with a squeaky hinge. "Cass sent you," I accused.

"*Nobody* sends me," boasted Mr. Macho Man. "I'm here because I hate snitches. You rat out those girls, and you'll be sorry."

He gave my hair another vicious yank. Kenny mim-

192

icked, " 'Hi, I'm back from Springfield because the meet was called off.' And you fell for it, you dumb-ass."

Jed hadn't called—it'd been Kenny mimicking him. Kenny, who was laughing his fool head off with B.K., both so smug that they thought they could scare me into silence. But suddenly I was not scared but flaming mad.

"So you hate snitches, huh?" I snarled back at B.K. "Well, why don't you ask Diana what she told me so's I'd keep quiet about Cass and Karen's little prank?" Kenny snuffled, what the hell did I mean? "Diana told me that you two jerks dug that ditch on Spruce Way. That you were so stupid you figured nobody'd guess it was you. That's what you are to Diana, Kenny. A dork with nice wheels."

"She's lying," B.K. snarled. He yanked my hair back again, but even pain couldn't keep me quiet.

"Diana told me about the night you two bozos chased me through the woods on Mountain Road. Yeah, B.K., she fingered you, too. How about that, huh? Diana was willing to deal—give you two up so's I'd keep quiet about Cass and Karen—"

"Shut *up* or I'll make you keep quiet," B.K. threatened. "You made all that up—"

Bright car lights weaved around the corner of Fern Way and came bobbing down the road. In the mini-second that B.K. turned to glance toward those lights, I kicked backward with all my might. His howl of pain came simultaneous to the crack of my heel contacting with his shin, and he was still yelling when I eeled out of his grip and sprinted back toward the house.

"You've crippled me—I'll *kill* you—" I didn't stick around to hear more but raced down the road. Gulping

193

for air, I reached the house just as Dad's car pulled up into the driveway beside me.

"What are you doing, breaking the school record for the hundred-yard dash?" he wanted to know. Then he added somberly, "Until this thing is over, Meg, I don't want you out running by yourself, especially at night."

Dad, if you only knew. I almost told him what had just happened, but then I held back. I knew that Dad would go after those slimeballs, but right now I was after bigger prey. See, Diana wasn't the only one who could play head games. Now that I'd told Kenny and B.K. about Diana's ratting on them, I wanted to wait and see what would happen.

Saturday, I was up at four to travel to the Springfield meet with the team. I saw Jed there, but I didn't have a chance to tell him more than the bare details of what happened before the meet. *After* the meet, everyone was too excited because one of our runners had placed third in the race. I told Jed I'd talk to him when he got home from Springfield, but he got home too late Sunday to call.

On Monday, school was buzzing with the news that Karen and Cass had been suspended. At lunch, Jed made me go over all the details of what had happened. He was really upset about Mimi and horrified about my encounter with Kenny and B.K. "I don't believe you—are you totally nuts? Why didn't you tell your dad?" he demanded.

I said I'd thought about it but decided to wait. "Kenny was really rattled," I began, then stopped short as Diana and Vi sauntered into the cafeteria.

194

Diana's strawberry-blond hair glinted in the light, and Vi looked stunning in white pants and a deep violet tee. Both girls were laughing and joking around. "Toughing it out," Jed muttered. "I guess Cass and Karen didn't tell the police anything about their pals."

Glumly, we watched the two girls move through the lunch line, talking and waving to kids they knew. They looked and acted as if they hadn't a care in the world, and if the code of silence held, there'd be no way to prove that there were four Hunters, not two. If all the Hunters hung tight, it would blow over.

"Don't they look as if they're feeling no pain?" Jed wondered disgustedly. Then he went, "Whoa—here comes Kenny, and he doesn't look like a happy camper."

We both watched as Kenny walked straight up to Diana. He said something to her that she brushed off. Then he said something else. "I don't *want* to talk to you about it, okay?" we heard her say. "Later, Kenny."

"Not later, now!" Kenny's voice rose. Diana started to walk around him, but he got in front of her.

Jed hopped to his feet and called across the lunch-room, "She sold you *out,* man!"

Shooting a furious glare at Jed, Diana started to walk forward. Kenny reached out and grabbed her arm to stop her, and as she tried to jerk free, the spaghetti on her plate took a flying leap and ended all over Kenny's shirt.

"Food fight!" somebody yelled.

A slice of pizza came sailing by us and hit a kid at the next table. He turned around and pitched his pie across the room. In a few seconds, bread, salad, bananas, and sandwiches commenced to fly around the cafeteria—

195

accompanied by shrieks of protest, laughter, and the yells of the lunch monitor.

"Sit tight," Jed counseled gleefully. Then he yelped as a big gob of chocolate pudding caught him in the chest. "Hey, watch it!"

Male teachers, monitors, and Mr. MacMasters himself came running. Food stopped flying as our principal yelled to Stop This Or You're All In Trouble. "Who started this?" he demanded.

"She did." Kenny was so mad he could hardly talk. "Diana."

"Shut up, you big jerk," Vi shouted. "It was an accident."

MacMasters marched Diana and Kenny off to his office, then told Vi to come along, too. "I said so, that's why," he bellowed when Vi protested. "Don't give me attitude. Move!"

"They've got trouble now," I exulted.

Jed said so did he, his mother would take a fit when she saw the mess on his shirt. Then he went, "But it's worth it. After what happened, I'll bet Kenny starts singing like a canary."

The thought of Kenny as a canary made me howl. Jed grinned, too. Then he said, "Supposing we go down to the police station after school and see Officer Oakes?"

But when we got there, we found the police officer totally frustrated, and after I'd introduced Jed, she told us why. "Kenny's agreed to cooperate with us, but what he tells us we can't use," she said. "Kenny doesn't really have any proof that the girls were engaged in any wrongdoing."

"He was the one who showed me that flyer Rea'd supposedly handed out," I pointed out.

"He swears he doesn't know who's responsible for that flyer. He maintains that he doesn't know anything about Rea. He also says that though he knew that the girls were tormenting you, Meg, he never actually *saw* them doing anything." Officer Oakes looked even more gloomy as she added, "Chasing Meg through the woods was Kenny's and B.K.'s idea. So was their digging the ditch on Spruce Way. So far it's the boys' wrongdoing, not Diana's."

"You mean, nothing will happen to Diana or Vi?" I cried. Officer Oakes said that was about the way it was.

"Hearsay won't hold up in court, and Diana Angeli has covered her tracks extremely well. Unless one of the other girls confesses, there's just no *proof*." Officer Oakes broke off to add bitterly, "Meanwhile, if you can believe this, Mr. Angeli's yelling harassment and threatening us with a lawsuit."

As she spoke the station's swinging outer door parted, and Mrs. Alvarez came walking in. Dressed all in black, she looked thinner than when I'd seen her last.

She glanced around the police station, saw Jed and me with Officer Oakes, and came over to greet us. Then, pulling some sheets of paper out of her purse, she handed them to Officer Oakes. "Just as you told me to on the phone, I have written down everything I can remember about how Diana Angeli tormented my Rea."

As if on cue, the swinging doors of the police station opened once again, and Mrs. Angeli walked in.

She looked stunning in fawn-colored wool slacks and matching cashmere cardigan. Behind her came Diana, followed by a chunky, grim-looking guy in a three-piece suit—Mr. Julius Angeli. Finally, at the end of the procession, was a graying man with a briefcase.

197

"Look at them," Jed said as the Angelis and their attorney marched down the corridor. "They act like they own the place."

"Diana!"

At Mrs. Alvarez's cry, there was a ripple in the approaching group. The phalanx never broke stride, but I saw Mr. and Mrs. Angeli both move closer to their daughter. Mr. Angeli snapped, "I know who you are. I'm warning you, stay away from my daughter."

"That is what *I* say to you long time ago, only you don't listen!"

Tears rode Mrs. Alvarez's voice. Officer Oakes leaned over and said something to her in a low voice. "I do not make trouble," Rea's mother declared. "I want only to ask this girl a question. *Why* did you hate my daughter?"

As if she hadn't heard, Diana turned her head away. She looked unconcerned, unmoved, the queen of cool. Meanwhile her father directed an impatient look at his attorney, who said, "This is an inappropriate discussion. My client is here to see Captain Harley."

They started to walk past us. "Tell me why you picked on Rea," Mrs. Alvarez yelled after them. "Was it because she wasn't pretty enough? Because she was Hispanic? Because her father is in jail? I have to know because I think of this all the time."

Her voice cracked on a sob. The Angelis' lawyer now said something about harassment. "Right—like Diana didn't harass Rea," Jed burst out. "Like she didn't do the same thing to Meg."

My cue. I took a deep breath and said, "I know why you got after *me,* Diana. It was because I was asking questions about what you and the others did to Rea, right?"

I began to detail the things the Hunters had done to me. Mr. CEO Julius Angeli stared at me, then turned to the police officers who'd drifted up and were listening. "Get these people out of our way," he directed. "My daughter has rights."

Nobody moved. "You should've been at Rea's funeral," I told Diana. "It was your fault she killed herself. You went after her. 'We're gonna get that Rea,' right?"

No response, but Diana's lips tightened. "Yeah, that's right, somebody saw you at your dumb little pajama party," I needled. "You wanted to bring Rea down, and you did." Silence. "Did you tell Cass to put the drugs in Rea's locker, or did you do it yourself?" Silence. "Did you put that knife in my book bag?" Silence—still silence. "You did, didn't you, Diana?"

"I don't have to listen to this crap."

Jerking her arm free from her mother, Diana turned and walked quickly back down the hall toward the swinging doors. I ran after her, crying, "Admit it, Diana, you tortured Rea until she killed herself."

Somebody grabbed my shoulder, spun me around, and I found myself eye to unfriendly eye with Mrs. Angeli. For one second, only. Then: "Let *go* of Meg," Mrs. Alvarez shouted.

She swooped down to my side, grabbed Mrs. Angeli by her expensive cashmere cardigan, and literally hauled her away. "You should be ashamed of having such a daughter," Mrs. Alvarez cried.

"You—you idiot! See what you've done!"

Mrs. Angeli fiddled with the sleeve of her cardigan, brushed and rubbed it, as if Mrs. Alvarez's touch had soiled the garment. "Julius, you saw how this woman attacked me," she snarled. "She's ruined my sweater. *Ruined* it."

"Oh, *Mother,*" Diana muttered, "will you get a grip?"

Mrs. Angeli glared at her daughter and hissed, "You shut your mouth! You got us into this mess, and now this madwoman's ruined my sweater. It's your fault, and I'll never forgive you, Diana."

"Damn you, *stop* it!"

Diana's voice was a harsh whisper. Her eyes were wide, and her hands worked as if they were wringing air. Twisting and choking air as she had once wrung those red-stained paper towels. "I *hate* you, do you hear me? All you care about is *you.* Your damned house, your stupid sweater. You never, not once, ever cared about *me.*"

"Diana," Mr. Angeli barked. "Stop this—now!"

Totally ignoring him, still staring at her mother, Diana cried, "We did it to Rea, okay? We drove her crazy."

Then the Angelis' attorney got a hold of Diana's arm and started to propel his client toward the door. Diana shrugged him away. "Why should I keep quiet? Leave me alone, you jerk—we *did* it. It was my idea. And it's over."

"It is *not* over."

The tears had dried on Mrs. Alvarez's cheeks, and she was breathing hard, as if she'd run a mile in record time. Her face was almost paper white. "I don't know about the law so much," she told Diana. "I don't know if the judge will even punish you and your friends, but I don't even care about that."

200

Then, as if she and Diana were all alone in the police station, she added almost gently, "I only pray that you will think of my Rea every single day of your life. As I will."

TWELVE

"MEG, WHEN ARE you going to see your grandmother?"

It was Saturday, the sun was shining, and I was putting on my running shoes. "Later," I said. "After my run, I'll go."

"After your run you'll remember you have homework, or perhaps you'll clean your room," my mother said. "You haven't been to see your grandmother in a week. It's not like you."

One of my shoelaces snapped in my hands. I threw it down, glaring at the shoelace as if I hated it.

"Don't do what I did, Meg," Mom was saying. "Don't avoid her because you can't face what's happening to her."

What hurts most has a grain of truth in it— "Why can't you leave me alone?" I snarled at Mom.

She paid no attention. "So many nights I pretended I was desperately needed at the store and left you to cope with Mama. Do you know why? Because I couldn't bear to see her deteriorating. That's why I put it all on you." Mom drew in a sighing breath, let it go. "Trouble was, even when I tried not to think about her, Mama was always in my mind."

"I still see her sitting by the side of the road," I mumbled.

Mom came into my room and sat down on my bed beside me. "It was so awful, Mom. I—I was *ashamed* of her. I didn't want to *be* there."

"I know, honey."

Hot, guilty tears squeezed my lids. I leaned my head against Mom's shoulder, and she stroked my hair. "Why did it have to happen, Mom?" I groaned. "I wish she'd never met Silky."

Silky, who was still in the CCU and fighting his own grim battle. "Sometimes I wish that, too." Mom paused uncertainly, her soft, plump face sad. "I know what you're thinking—maybe if she hadn't cared for him and hadn't seen him stricken, she'd be okay. But who's to say that either of *them* would have wanted that? It was a rare friendship they had, Meg, and they are braver than I'll ever be."

Braver than me, too, I wanted to say. Because what would have happened that day if I'd gone into Rea's house, talked to her, shown her she had at least one friend? I had to face the unwanted answer: maybe I could have saved her life, and everything would've been different.

"We do the best we can," Mom said, and for a second I thought I'd spoken my thoughts aloud. Then she added, "Anyway, I wanted to tell you that you're not alone in feeling the way you do, Meg."

When she'd gone, I sat for a long time before taking off my running shoes and sliding on my sneakers. I was tempted to call Jed and ask him to meet me at Meadowriver, but I knew that I couldn't do that. I couldn't risk Jed seeing Mimi the way she'd been last Friday.

As I biked along the loops and turns of Mountain

Road, I tried to prepare myself for what I'd find at Meadowriver. Not that I was any more prepared an hour later when the staff member on duty looked up with a smile and said, "We haven't seen you around for a few days, Meg. What's happening?"

"Not much," I said, adding, "How is she?"

"Asleep when I looked in on her earlier this morning. I'm sure she'll be glad to see you."

I went down the first-floor hallway. In the rec room, Mr. Saito was playing checkers with another old guy, and I could hear Ms. Pors's unmistakable bellow. Nothing had changed except for the silent piano, and I passed the room in a hurry.

The hallway, splashed as it was with morning sun, felt oppressive without Mimi's music. Still, the atrium was practically smothered with chrysanthemums, and members of the First-Floor Club were walking or caning and wheeling themselves about to enjoy the morning. Nurses were busy dispensing medication, and Ruth broke her stride long enough to wave at me.

"How is she?" I asked.

"In and out." Ruth stopped, gave me a level stare. "Don't be upset if you see a change, Meg. It's the medication she's on."

"Will she be all right again?" I asked.

"Sure she will." Ruth gave me a friendly little pat on the shoulder. "Go on over to her room—she'll be glad to see you."

I slowly went across the hall to the room and stood there staring at the words MARGARET S. CASTLEWAY, 112-B for several long minutes. Then I drew a deep breath and went in. The bed next to Mimi's was empty. Mimi, dressed neatly in pale beige slacks and a pink sweater, was lying down on hers.

Lying down in the middle of the morning. Her eyes closed, her fingers resting heavily on her flat stomach. Her lips moving once in a while, as if trying to remember something in her sleep, and at her feet the blue quilt she'd brought with her to Meadowriver.

"Mimi?" I whispered.

Unhearing, she slumbered on. Never mind about facing hard truths, I'd hoped that she'd be up and clear-eyed, that the fog would have been gone from her mind.

"Like I said, she's in and out." Ruth had followed me into the room. She walked over to the bed and gave Mimi's arm a little shake. "Mimi?" she said loudly, cheerfully. "Meg's here to see you."

Mimi just lay there. "It's the medication, like you told me," I said, trying to find excuses. "I—I'll just sit here for a while."

Ruth left and I sat by the bed watching Mimi's fine-boned face and trying to wish her healthy again. I took her hand in mine, but it lay limp and unresponsive, and unable to stand the silence, I began to talk.

It was like the one-sided dinner conversations we'd had so often. "Jed sends his love, Mimi. When's he coming? Next week, for sure. I just wanted to have you to myself today. And, Mimi, the Hunters are in deep trouble now that Diana's confessed."

I told Mimi that I had a feeling that Diana hadn't confessed out of guilt and remorse, as her attorney was making out, but because she'd wanted to hurt her mother by creating this awful, disorderly scandal. Diana'd finally found a way to make Mrs. Angeli pay.

"Anyway, the Angelis' attorney has convinced her that she should make a special deal with the police. I guess Cass and Vi got the same advice from *their* lawyers, because there's been a lot of ratting and finger-pointing going on. Awful, huh?"

Silent and unresponsive, Mimi dreamed on. I tried again, recounting that Kenny and B.K. had been suspended from school for a week, and that B.K. had been kicked off the football team. Also, due to Diana's confession, she, Cass, and Vi and Karen had been arraigned in court. Cass and Karen were charged with possession of drugs.

"All of them are accused of causing mental anguish," I told Mimi. "I don't think they'll go to jail. Probably they'll be given probation, except Diana. I guess her lawyer fixed it so that all she'll have to do is community service. It doesn't seem fair, does it? I mean, she started doing all this stuff, and she ratted everybody out, and she comes out smelling like roses."

Except, she'd have to deal with her mother. "And Karen's going to go away to live with her father," I said, then paused to rub my thumb across Mimi's knuckles. "I think it'll be good for her to be away from Mrs. Tierney, right? If her mom hadn't been so strict with her, I don't think Munch'd ever have started hanging out with the Hunters—"

I broke off as Mimi opened her eyes. She looked at me, blinked several times, and my heart tightened with hope as she focused on my face. "Hiya," I said around the lump in my throat.

"How nice to see you," my grandmother murmured politely. "How kind of you to come."

She didn't know me. "It's Meg," I said urgently. Then,

making a joke of it, I quavered: "How could you forget your one and only granddaughter?"

"Meg?" She looked bewildered. "But she's just a little girl. You must be mistaken—" She broke off, closed her eyes again. "I'm very tired."

She hadn't even *known* me. Unable to stand the thought, I got up and walked stiff-legged out into the hall. How could Mimi have forgotten me? "I'd have remembered *you*," I whispered, and the tears scalded down my cheeks. I brushed them away, but they spilled down again. "I'd never have forgotten *you*."

Ruth was standing at the other end of the hall. I didn't want to talk to her right now. What I wanted to do was get away, get *out* of there. Blinking tears out of my eyes, I started walking quickly down the hall and the atrium. I was hurrying past the rec room on my way to the front door when I heard an unmusical sound. Someone was trying to play the piano.

Ms. Pors was frowning down at the keys, picking at them with one finger. I quickened my step, but I wasn't fast enough.

"Meg!" she boomed. "Aren't you coming over to say hello?"

I mumbled, oh, hello, and added that I was in a hurry, but there was no escaping Ms. Pors. "Just come over here for a minute," she bellowed. "I need some help with this."

She was squinting at a sheet of music, and as I reluctantly drew nearer I recognized the first piece Mimi'd ever taught me, "The Happy Farmer."

"Your grandmother was teaching me to play this tune, lamb," Ms. Pors complained, "and then she had her setback." She squinted nearsightedly up at me. "She said you know the piece."

"It was a long time ago," I protested, but Ms. Pors wasn't buying it.

"You haven't lived long enough for there to *be* a long time ago, lamb," she boomed. "Fifty years, seventy years, *that's* long. Now, sit down here, lamb, and play this for me."

Reluctantly, wanting to be anywhere but there but not knowing how to get out of it, I squeezed myself onto the piano bench beside Ms. Pors. "I don't know if I can do this," I mumbled.

Ms. Pors folded her hands and waited and I tried not to think of how often I'd sat next to Mimi, looked sideways into a faintly quizzical face with fine bones and eyes the color of crushed spring violets. "Your hand's too tense," I could almost hear Mimi say. "Visualize a flower in your palm. Hold it so it won't fall, but don't crush it. So."

Now she no longer knew me. I wanted to go someplace and cry but— "Go ahead and play," bellowed Ms. Pors. "What are you waiting on, lamb?"

I pressed down on the keys and the first notes slid apologetically into the rec room. I forced out the next and the next until my fingers remembered their cues and began to move on their own, cautiously bringing to life the cheerful little tune Ms. Pors had been trying to play.

Conversation stilled, and I saw Mr. Saito turn to look at me. "There, you see? You've forgotten nothing," bawled Ms. Pors. "Once the music's inside your head, lamb, it stays there forever."

Slowly, by twos and threes, the First-Floor Club had begun to drift into the rec room. Sunlight slanted on canes and walkers, and in the silence that fell at the end of my playing, I could hear wheezing and grunts and the creaks of old bones.

"You heard about Silky, huh?" Ms. Pors asked. "He's still in the CCU at the hospital, lamb. We heard there was a lot of damage to the heart—a *lot* of damage. If he comes back here, he'll be on the second floor, I expect. Well, well, I guess that's where we're all headed."

If she kept this up, I'd start crying again and not be able to stop. In instinctive self-defense my fingers started to brush the keys, slipping along an old, old tune.

Mimi's lullaby. It brought so many memories—like the way she wrinkled her nose when she laughed. The way her eyes sparkled when she was making a point. Her firm touch on my shoulder, her salty jokes, and those Regency sayings she loved to shock people with. A hundred memories, funny and good, about a different woman from a different life. A woman who now didn't even know me.

I stopped playing. There was scattered applause, and Ms. Pors threw a massive arm around me and mashed my ribs. "Now, *that* wasn't so hard, was it? You played it almost as well as your grandmother. So sweet, but sad, too, lamb. Why not play something happier?"

She looked around the room for confirmation and Mr. Saito cleared his throat. "The player is different but the music lives on," he intoned. "A thing of beauty never dies. Play 'Beautiful Dreamer,' Meg."

Channel your emotion, Meg—the stranglehold around my heart eased a little as I started to play one of Mimi's favorite tunes. Behind me and beside me I heard the rasps and coughs as old folks drifted close and began to tune up their ancient throats.

"Bee-yoo-tiful dreamer, awaken to me-ee," shrieked

Ms. Pors. Mr. Saito sang gamely along, off-key, and Miss Harriway let loose with a quavery soprano. The rest of the First-Floor Club hummed or rasped or screeched or growled out the words. Together, they sounded like a flock of wounded geese. Bloody, Mimi might say, but unbowed.

The members of the First-Floor Club knew that they were fighting a powerful enemy who was going to win in the end. That wasn't going to stop them. Bring him along, produce him, and they'd sing right in Death's face.

They were all so brave that they made me feel brave, too. Brave enough to go back to Mimi's room. And then what? I asked myself. What next, Meg?

Because from here on out it wasn't going to be enough merely to cheer her on from the sidelines. If I truly loved her, I would have to run beside Mimi in this last, dark race.

Could I do it? I wasn't sure. Was my newfound courage going to be enough? I didn't know that either, but I was going to do my best. I was really going to try to run the distance with her.

So today, after I finished playing for the First-Floor Club, I knew that I'd go back to Mimi's room and sit with her until she woke up again. If she knew me—wonderful. If she didn't, I would still be there.

Together, I promised my grandmother, *as long as it takes, wherever it takes us.* And my pledge swelled with her music to fill my heart.

Look for this moving book
by Maureen Wartski:

CANDLE IN THE WIND

When Harris Mizuno, a Japanese-American
teenager, is shot by an elderly white man, only Terri,
his sister, can keep the family together.

For a glimpse of this book,
please turn the page . . .

CANDLE IN THE WIND
by Maureen Wartski

"WHY WOULD SOMEONE shoot Harris?"

"It has to be a mistake!"

Alice and I cried out at the same time. Our voices entwined, shrilled up, and then disappeared into the sound of drumming rain.

"What is this? What do you mean, my son's been shot?" Dad strode past Mom and into the rain toward the policeman. He sounded incredulous. "He just went down to the store."

The cop just said, "Please come with me, sir. I'll take you straight to Xavier Hospital."

"But what *happened*? Can't you tell us how badly hurt he is?" Mom cried. "He's going to be all right, isn't he?"

Once more the policeman repeated, "Please come with me to the hospital, ma'am."

"It's bad—oh, it has to be," Emily Blankard speculated in an uncharacteristically hushed voice. My mind started to scramble around in wild directions. Maybe Harris had interrupted a burglary in progress. Maybe he'd got caught in some kind of drug shootout. Maybe—

Mom said, "Oh, dear God," in a choked voice, started forward, then swayed as if she were going to faint. Dad just stood there looking stunned, but Art Blankard reached out and grabbed Mom's arm.

"You and Jun go ahead, Laura," he rumbled. "I'll bring the kids."

As if his voice had unloosed everybody from paralysis, people began to explode into talk, explaining things to each other over and over as if they couldn't take it in. Harris had been shot—yes, shot! God alone knew why, or by whom, and nobody knew how seriously he'd been hurt—

Into this commotion Alice wailed, "Len—what's happened to Len?"

I'd totally forgotten that Len Kamemoto had gone with Harris. The policeman cleared his throat. "Mr. Kamemoto was taken to Xavier Hospital, too." Then he opened the cruiser door for our parents.

Dad walked, stiff legged, to the squad car. He looked as if he were sleepwalking. Mom started to follow, turned distractedly back to us.

"Art will bring the children, Laura," Emily Blankard cried. "You go on, now, dear, and don't worry about us. We're all praying for you."

We watched Mom and Dad drive on ahead as we climbed into Art Blankard's sturdy Buick station wagon. Art switched on his high beams and put the pedal to the metal, all without saying a word.

He didn't open his mouth again till we reached the emergency entrance of Xavier Hospital, and then all he said was, "My money's on Harris. He's tough— he'll make it."

All the way to the hospital, I'd repeated a single prayer. Let Harris be okay, I'd promised the Lord, and I would never ever do anything remotely sinful again. I imagine that Alice had been on the same wavelength because she grabbed my hand as we raced for the emergency entrance. "They have to be all right," she whimpered.

213

Mitch had wrapped himself in tense silence that he now broke. "Maybe Harris is just, you know, wounded, not—"

Not dead. Somewhere I'd read that it was bad luck to talk of death in a hospital. I pinched Mitch's arm and hissed, "Don't say it," so fiercely that he shut up.

The emergency-room receptionist directed us to another room where our folks were waiting. In a corner by the window, two police officers were talking in low tones to Len Kamemoto. Len looked stunned, and his shirt was covered with blood.

"Len," Alice yelped, and started to cross the room toward him, but Dad looked up sharply.

"Leave him alone," he commanded. "The police are talking to him just now."

"Harris?" I pleaded. My mom didn't react, but Dad replied that Harris was in surgery and that the doctors were doing all they could.

"They have the best technology, the best surgeons." Dad spoke the words firmly, as if trying to convince himself. Beside him, Mom gave a hoarse sob. She looked smaller than ever, scrunched back into the waiting room's fake-leather seat. "Oh, children," she whispered, groping for us.

Her hand felt icy. "A man shot Harris when he went to the door. *Shot* my boy," she repeated, in disbelief. "The bullet lodged near the heart."

It couldn't be real. Mom began to sob, and the policemen with Len straightened up. One of them snapped shut a notebook and said, "That about does it for now. We'll need you to come down to the station to make a formal statement, Mr. Kamemoto." Len nodded, not looking up, and mumbled something I couldn't catch. "Fine," the cop said. "Later this evening would be fine."

He looked toward us, seemed as if he wanted to say some word of comfort, then changed his mind and went out quietly, trailed by his partner. Len stayed where he was.

Alice let go of Mom's hand and ran over to Len, dropped on her knees beside him. "Are you okay? Len, what *happened*?"

Before Len could answer, Dad jerked around to stare at him. "Tell us what you told the police," he directed sternly. "First, what were you doing in the center of town? I thought you were going to the convenience store on the corner."

Len blinked sickly up at us. "The corner grocery was out of mayo, so Harris said we should drive to the Stop and Save in Hanley. My car started acting up just as we passed the town square, and then we drove past the park onto North Street and through the wooded area where the road curves around and around—"

"What does it matter if the road winds or not?" I blurted. "Who shot Harris? A robber, or a mugger, or what?"

"Waring," our mother said dully. "The man's name is Rodney Waring."

"Have the cops *arrested* him?" Mitch almost shouted, and Dad told him to keep his voice down, this was a hospital.

"Let Len speak," he said. "Don't interrupt."

Everybody looked at Len, who said, "My car died in that wooded area on North Street. We tried getting it started, but it wouldn't turn over. The starter, I think—"

"Never *mind* that," Dad snapped, but Len wasn't to be hurried. As if he were sleepwalking through his memory, he described seeing a house set back from the road, half-hidden by trees.

"Harris said he'd go ask the people in the house if he could use the phone," Len muttered. The pallor in his face had begun to tinge with green as he added, "Harris

215

ran down the road and up the driveway and knocked. No-body came to the door, so he knocked again. I heard him shouting something. And then the door opened and I heard this, ah, this *blast*—"

Len made a gulping sound, jumped up from his chair, and ran, half-doubled up and choking, toward the men's room. Alice dropped her face into her hands. Mom said in a stunned voice, "This Waring shot my boy just because he came to the door of his house. What kind of monster would do that?"

"A criminal," Dad said through clenched teeth. "He'll pay for this. Attempted murder is—"

"Mr. and Mrs. Mizuno?"

The swinging doors to our left had parted, and a green-coated doctor came into the room. He looked tired and sad, and suddenly, everything in the room went quiet. Dad squared his shoulders and got up, stood straight, almost to attention. "Yes," he said. "Yes, doctor."

Mom shrank back into her chair, and Alice put her arms around her. Mitch edged toward me, and we clasped hands.

Knowing what was to come, knowing in my bones but praying, still, I gave God a last chance. Please, I thought, let Harris be all right. Please, *please*—

"I'm sorry," the doctor said. "I'm so sorry. We did the best we could for your son, but we lost him."

CANDLE IN THE WIND
by Maureen Wartski

Published by Fawcett Books
Available in your local bookstore.